The KEY to EVERYTHING

BEVERLY VARNADO

The Key to Everything
By Beverly Varnado
© Copyright 2018 Beverly Varnado

Published by Anaiah Romance
An imprint of Anaiah Press, LLC.
7780 49th ST N. #129
Pinellas Park, FL 33781

First Anaiah Romance ebook edition September 2018
Edited by Kara Leigh Miller
Book Design by Laura Heritage
Cover Design by Laura Heritage

Anaiah Press | A Mighty Presence

To my friends at Rays Church, who know the power of God's love and forgiveness.

ACKNOWLEDGEMENTS

My deepest thanks...

To my husband, Jerry, for this wonderful life we have together. I love you more. Also for the legal advice for the character of David.

To my dear family, Aaron, Bethany, Mari, Brent, Walker, and Sara Alden. To my sister and best friend, Tammy, Foy, and Christopher.

To Dr. Marni Dodd, for the medical assistance for Genny's character.

To my mom, who sees from heaven.

To my spiritual mentors, Dr. Warren and Jane Lathem, Rev. Grady and Doris Wigley, Dr. Gary and Diane Whetsone, Rev. Walton and Martha McNeal.

To my wonderful readers at One Ringing Bell.

To the precious friends in my writing group. So grateful for you.

Remembering my beloved dad, Steve Chitwood (1928-2015).

CHAPTER ONE

TIRES CRUNCHED ON THE GRAVEL DRIVEWAY outside Genny Sanders's house, and a car door slammed. Her handyman, Al Trenton, hadn't had time to go home, get his lawn mower, and come back to mow her grass, so she stepped to the door and, as a precaution, latched the screen. People in Worthville didn't lock their doors, but it was hard to shake her New York sensibilities. Her stomach tightened a bit as a handsome man in his thirties holding a briefcase approached. Had she forgotten an appointment? Who was this tall, trim guy in an expensive suit?

"Sorry to disturb, but are you Dr. Genevieve Sanders?"

"I am." She brushed bangs from her face and hoped she didn't have packing peanuts in her ponytail. A broad smile eased across his face, disarming Genny with its charm, but she regained the game face she'd learned to have as a medical professional. "May I help you?"

"I'm David Worth, attorney and executor of your

grandmother's estate." He extended his business card.

Genny read the card through the screen and nodded. "Of course. We spoke on the phone. I'm sorry. With all the moving drama, I'd forgotten you were coming by. Call me Genny." She unlatched the screen door and opened it for him. As she did, one of the hinges snapped, and the door sagged. She sighed. "I have a few repairs to make." Her grandmother had been without much help for a couple of years since Al's father, Lester, died. Al had retired from his factory job in recent weeks and stepped in to help. "I haven't made much progress unpacking. I've only been in town three days. As I told you on the phone when we scheduled this appointment, I came for the funeral when my grandmother died two months ago, but I had to go back to New York right after, until the doctor I worked for could find my replacement." Why was she rambling? Must be moving exhaustion. She gestured toward the sofa. "Have a seat if you can find one."

David moved a box from her grandmother's comfortable old sofa and took a seat.

Genny eased onto the wingback. "Not many lawyers make house calls these days. "

"Small town, you know. We do what it takes." David squirmed in his seat and unbuttoned his jacket, seeming to grow uncomfortable. He ran a hand through his black hair, which held a slight curl. "I won't keep you long, but before you get too far with your unpacking, I thought I'd make you aware of a situation." He cleared his throat. "Saul Lance, a developer here in Worthville, has put together a land parcel for development. He plans to make Worthville a retirement destination. It's close enough to Atlanta and the cultural advantages there, yet these houses would cost far less than a similar one in the Atlanta market. We expect it to be a huge success."

Genny leaned back in her chair and shrugged. "How does that affect me?" She slid a magazine off an end table and fanned herself.

David cleared his throat. "Lance needs more land for his development."

Genny couldn't imagine what this might have to do with her and meant to convey that through her "So what?" look. She put the magazine in her lap and twirled her ponytail, waiting for an explanation.

David opened his briefcase and took out a paper, which appeared to be a plat. He pointed to an area. "The project is planned for this area." He circled an area on the plat with his finger. "Your fifteen acres sits where he's planned the grand entrance with his clubhouse and pool."

Genny sat erect in her chair as she understood David's suggestion. "My property is not for sale."

David shifted in his seat, and a bead of perspiration tracked down his face. He took out a monogrammed handkerchief and wiped his face. "You might not want to make that decision in haste. Since he needs your land to proceed, he'd be willing to pay top dollar."

"Mr. Worth, this is where my grandmother raised me." Genny stood in defiance. *Who does this man think he is?* "I'm not about to sell out to some quick-money developer who wants to build a bunch of McMansions."

"I thought before you established roots, you'd—"

"These *are* my roots."

David rose.

Genny stepped face to face with David. "You were my grandmother's estate executor and her lawyer." She edged even closer. "How long has this been going on? Have you been representing her interests or Mr. Lance's? Looks like you've had a conflict of interest." Genny pivoted, moved to the door, and held it open.

David mumbled something like "Call me if you change your mind," strode to his car, and spun out of the yard, leaving a plume of Georgia red clay dust in his wake. Goodness, she hoped this wasn't a foreshadowing of what life was going to be like in Worthville. The nerve of him, thinking he could march in and negotiate her right out of the home her grandmother left her. As the dust settled in the yard, she tried to let her flurry of emotions settle by relaxing her rigid posture and unfurling her fingers.

Genny turned, took a deep breath, and moved around the room, surveying the furnishings. She'd spent many an evening in this room, working on homework while her grandmother read. She stopped at the green striped wing chair, caressing its back, noticing her grandmother's well-used Bible on the table. Her grandmother's faith was constant, yet her own faith...well, not so much. A mystery from one of her grandmother's favorite authors also lay on the table. Genny lifted the novel, noting the bookmark her grandmother used to mark her place, the last words she'd read—the last mystery.

She moved to the fireplace and gazed at a landscape painting hanging above it. Her grandmother painted it long ago from a spot at the base of the back stairs. She recognized the scene by how the fences lined the pastures behind the house. This picture, created by the hands of the woman who meant so much to her, magnified Genny's sense of loss, causing that old, familiar ache to rise in her heart again.

She pulled her T-shirt away from her sticky body and shook it to wave cooler air next to her skin, and then turned on a fan sitting between open side windows. With the early-summer heat beginning to build and her grandmother never having central air-conditioning installed, it would be something to get used to, for sure. Maybe she'd buy a window unit or two.

Genny spied Al rolling back into the yard. He declined the offer to use her old push mower. She believed his exact words had been "Ain't used a push mower since Reagan was in office." She called to him through the screen, "When you start mowing, be careful of the chicken."

As if on cue, her grandmother's beloved hen, Elizabeth, flapped onto the gray painted wooden porch. The hen strutted around a moment before Genny stepped outside and scooped her into her arms. "Don't worry, girl. You'll be safe." Elizabeth eyed her almost as if the bird understood what she said. She deposited her on the porch, and the chicken continued her patrol as if surveying her kingdom from the porch.

Genny went back inside to unpack boxes, and in her peripheral vision, Al glided by on what appeared to be a new mower—not a small one either. Looked like one of those heavy-duty models. Expensive. How could he afford a new mower like that? She grabbed a box cutter to open a box near the sofa and thought of David sitting there trying to manipulate her out of her inheritance. Was Worthville named after David Worth's family back somewhere along the line? Maybe he thought he could do anything he wanted to because he bore the same name as the town.

"We'll see about that," she said aloud. Then she sliced through the tape and tore open the box.

After unpacking most of the boxes in the living room, she needed to take a break from the back-breaking bending. She wandered out into the yard. Al had mentioned the gutters needed cleaning and that she had a tree growing in one of them. She didn't see how that was possible, but when she stood under the shade of the old magnolia and looked up, there it was. Just over the right corner of the wide front porch, a small Georgia pine sapling sprouted from the gutter. How long had it been since the gutters were cleaned? One more job she needed to take care of.

She faced regular upkeep with things like gutter cleaning in addition to repairs just because the house was old. Decades ago, her grandfather had built the original two-story central part of the house and then over the years added one-story wings on either side. Dormers topped the additions, giving the appearance of having a second story over them, making the house seem bigger than it was, but they merely balanced the outside, as there was no access to the space there.

Not a big house, and not worth much on the market. Few people wanted to live out here. Well, up until now anyway. David Worth told another story.

This house was her salvation when she was a child—and her grandmother's last gift to her. She'd never let it go. Never. Some slick-talking, albeit nice-looking, lawyer was not about to cause that to happen.

Nice-looking and slick-talking were Kurt's calling cards too, and where did that take her?

Calamity.

CHAPTER TWO

ROUND FOUR IN THE AFTERNOON, AL rode up on his mower, cut the ignition, and stepped onto the porch.

Genny opened the door, and Al handed her the shed keys as he wiped his forehead with a red bandana. An aura of fresh-cut grass surrounded him, reminding her of how his dad, Lester, used to smell after an afternoon mowing. It felt comfortable having Al around since Lester had been almost like a member of the family.

"Mighty hot out there—a lot of grass. I would've never made it pushin'."

"That's a nice mower." Genny pointed to the equipment in the yard. "Looks new."

"Five years old."

"Wow. Good condition." Genny didn't know much about lawn mowers, except how to turn them on, but Al's appeared to be pristine.

Al shifted his gaze to the hinge that broke earlier and fiddled with the metal appendage. "After I take my little granddaughter, Lori, to summer day camp in the morning, I'll be over here first thing to fix that. Those hinges have probably been on this door since the Flood, so it's no surprise they've done wore out. Make a list; I'll take care of whatever else you need too."

Genny nodded and laughed at Al's figure of speech about the Flood. Her grandmother used to refer to anything old as being around since the Flood—Noah's flood. She even referred to herself as being old as the Flood a time or two.

Al tipped his baseball hat. "See you tomorrow, then." He stomped back out in the yard, she guessed to load his lawn mower into the back of the truck. But before he did, he took a rag from his back pocket and wiped the mower from front to back. Could have been an Italian sports car for all the care he took. No wonder it looked as if it rolled off the hardware-store floor.

She moved to her grandmother's key box and dropped the shed keys into it. A wisp of cedar from the box floated in the air. She lifted a shiny brass key with a red ribbon attached and studied it. She'd seen it when she first gave Al the keys and wondered what it fit. Loud knocking interrupted her train of thought.

"Hello, hello. Is anyone there?"

Genny never remembered having so many visitors back when she lived with her grandmother. A woman about her age with straight brown hair, wearing an orange sundress and holding a pineapple, stood on Genny's porch. She looked like an advertisement for a fruit drink.

Genny stepped out, and her visitor placed the

prickly pineapple in her hands. "You must be Agnes's granddaughter, Genny. She told me so much about you. I'm a terrible cook, but I thought anyone would like a pineapple."

Genny laughed at the woman's honesty. "I do love pineapple." She motioned to the porch swing. Elizabeth had a penchant for laying eggs on the swing, so Genny checked it first before they took a seat. She put the pineapple on a table that had usually held a vase of flowers when her grandmother was alive.

Her guest pointed to the farmhouse on their left. "I'm Catherine Todd, the neighbor across the road. It's good to see something moving over here. I sure do miss Agnes."

Genny nodded as she put the swing in motion with her foot. "Me too."

Catherine turned to her. "She was one of my favorite people in the world. I'd grown up in Atlanta, but when I married Don, he wanted to move back to Worthville and landed a job here in management at the factory. I'd never lived in the country before, so I went through a bit of culture shock. You know, rolling fields instead of asphalt. Cows mooing instead of horns honking. Shopping at Harry's Hardware instead of Lenox Square."

Genny stopped the swing a moment. "Though I spent my childhood here, after my time in the city, I can understand why it'd be hard to adjust." When she'd first arrived in New York, it looked like another world to her—all the noise contrasted with the serenity of the country life she had known. Catherine probably experienced the same thing, only in reverse.

Catherine nodded. "Anyway, when we had the kids, I would sometimes feel isolated. Agnes saved me. I'd be about to pull my hair out with two toddlers, and she'd come over and play with them—even get on the floor." Catherine paused and glanced at her house. "How she did that at her age, I'll never know. She'd make up a story, do all the voices, and before long, she'd have us laughing."

Genny grinned. "Did she ever tell you the one about the five little groundhogs?"

"You mean the ones with—"

"—termites in their burrow." Genny finished her sentence.

They both burst into laughter.

Then Catherine put her hand on her mouth. "Am I talking too much? I guess I get desperate for adult conversation staying with small children all the time."

Genny placed her hand on Catherine's arm. "I love it. I've missed the easy way complete strangers in the South can connect with each other. After living in the North these past ten years, it's nice to let my guard down a little. But I don't consider you a stranger since you were my grandmother's friend. Chat away."

"Thank you," Catherine said as the chicken popped up on the porch. "Can you believe she rescued Elizabeth from the roadside?"

Genny nodded. "Elizabeth is one in a long succession of rescued chickens. It's almost like she possessed radar to know when a hen fell off one of those chicken transportation trucks. I laugh every time I think of Grandmother driving around in her car with yard fowl in the back seat." Because Elizabeth survived falling off a truck, her grandmother decided she should be a queen. Always called her the royal old bird. Grandmother Agnes was one of a kind. Tiny in stature but with a huge heart. Genny smiled at the memory with a warmth of affection.

Genny leaned forward and whispered, "Do you know, one weekend when I was visiting, I caught her taking one of them for a drive to the convenience store on a Sunday afternoon, and I'm pretty sure that was not an isolated occurrence."

Catherine put her hand to her mouth again. "No kidding."

Genny leaned back and swatted at a fly. "No kidding. She said the chickens deserved pampering after what they'd been through." Her grandmother did have her eccentricities. Genny turned to the carport her grandmother added to the house. Her grandmother's old luxury sedan was still out there. What would she do with it? Sell it, she imagined. She for sure couldn't see herself riding around in that car.

Catherine pointed to the pineapple on the table. "So what are you going to do with it? Are you a fabulous cook like your grandmother?"

Genny scrutinized the fruit. "Didn't get the gene. I'll chop it in pieces and take it for lunch."

Catherine smiled. "That's what I'd do. I heard you were the new nurse practitioner at Dr. Fleming's office."

"I am. Looking forward to it. When I happened to see the advertisement from Dr. Fleming about the nurse practitioner opening, I couldn't believe the timing. It was perfect."

Catherine's eyes narrowed, and she tilted her head as if puzzled. "I'm not sure I..."

"Long story. Sorry. It's just—the job couldn't have come at a better time."

"Anyway, we're glad you're here. Dr. Fleming could use the help. Always a long wait at his office. Good to know that will be changing." Catherine's brow furrowed; then her eyes widened. "Hey, the Zinnia Festival is this weekend. Why don't we go together? My husband has to work that day."

The Zinnia Festival. She hadn't been in years. She remembered it as one of the biggest and most fun events in Worthville. She'd love to go, but she yearned to be through with her moving chores so it wouldn't feel as if she was working two jobs all the time. "Thanks, but I have a lot of unpacking and organizing I need to get done."

"Why don't I come over Friday night and help after Don gets home? That way, you'll have a little time Saturday."

That might work. She could sure use the help, and she'd like to attend the festival. "All right, then. See you Friday night."

THAT EVENING, AS GENNY finished unpacking her books, a photograph fluttered from one to the floor. She retrieved it, an image of herself with a man standing in front of a sculpture in Central Park, and that old familiar anger surfaced, making her clinch her jaw. When she thought she was done with the past, something would happen, and all the feelings would flood back in. She thought moving back to Worthville would make them go away.

So far it hadn't.

The sculpture, called *Still Hunt*, was a depiction of a crouching panther ready to pounce. It often scared uninitiated park joggers. How prophetic to have their picture taken there, almost a foreshadowing of what was to come. She tore the photo in pieces and threw it in the trash can.

CHAPTER THREE

GENNY AND CATHERINE INCHED THEIR WAY along busy Main Street in Catherine's minivan, searching for a parking spot. "I anticipated it would be crazy, but this crowd looks larger than last year," Catherine said from the driver's seat.

In the back, four-year-old Lauren, with her mother's brown hair and blue eyes, was quite animated. "Mama, let's stop. I see the petting zoo."

Three-year-old John, more subdued, with dark eyes, perhaps like his father, Don, repeated, "Soo, soo."

"We'll go. Just try to be patient. We have to find a parking space."

They passed the one-hundred-year-old depot, renovated into a community center when the train company changed its route and ceased making stops in Worthville. The depot sat squarely in the middle of what had become, in recent years, a storybook town.

"Before I left for New York, Worthville fell on hard times when big-box stores began their encroachment.

Small Worthville businesses closed their doors, and for a time, it appeared the town might only be a place to gas up the car. But something happened after I left for college."

"The town came back to life?"

"Yes. My grandmother told me families began moving to Worthville for the quieter environment and sense of community."

Catherine stopped to let a family with three children cross the road. "Like we did."

"Exactly. Grandmother said though many worked in Perdue, they were willing to drive the extra miles to have Worthville for their home. With their arrival came the resources that spurred a revival of sorts."

Catherine nodded and pointed to a store down the street from the depot. Connie's Coffee and Cones boasted a sign in the window offering 20 percent off today for festival goers. "Yum, we'll have to stop by." She turned to Genny. "You have to meet Connie. She's incredible. She has the best ice cream you've ever tasted." Catherine paused a moment. "Her lattes aren't bad either."

Though Genny had made a point to visit her grandmother two or three times a year, the trips were short, and they never ventured out much. Genny was usually so exhausted from work, she just wanted to stay at home with her grandmother. Other than a quick trip to Gray's Grocery or church, they never went shopping, and she never really noticed the businesses very much when she came into town. It would be nice to meet or reacquaint herself with some of the people and places in

Worthville.

"Ice cream," echoed a tiny wistful voice from the back seat.

Genny turned to see Lauren gazing with longing at the ice cream store.

On the side street behind Connie's, Genny spotted the turn-of-the-century church her grandmother had attended. It was built with a bell tower, and Genny had long admired the architecture. Other than a fancy sign out front, nothing about it had changed. The digital display struck her as progressive for Worthville. She never found a church in Manhattan and got out of the habit of regular attendance. After what happened in the past year, it seemed to her God might be on vacation anyway.

Genny shifted her attention to the awning-covered front windows of Tucker's Tomes, where an author sat inscribing books. Even though her grandmother's house teemed with books, Genny loved nothing more than browsing bookstore shelves, even if she didn't buy anything.

Next door, Clyde's Cleaners urged festival goers to "Get a Zing out of the Zinnia Festival by Cleaning with Clyde." Genny thought Clyde might have stepped out onto a marketing limb with that angle, but nonetheless, he was doing a brisk business, judging by the number of customers coming and going.

Catherine giggled at the sign. "You know, it was Clyde who started the whole alliterative naming frenzy. People latched on to the concept, and next thing you know, you couldn't walk two steps without getting hit in the face with a stylistic literary device."

Genny remembered the business used to be called Worthville Cleaners. Clyde must have changed the name.

As they continued their slow progress down Main Street, Gray's Grocery occupied the next space in town. Genny wondered whether Gray bought the supermarket, which used be The Worthville Grocery, because his name went so well with *Grocery* or whether the Grays happened to already be in the grocery business. In any event, they were running a super special on cantaloupes this week. Since Genny arrived in Worthville, canned soup, power bars, and peanut butter on stale crackers had sustained her. She needed to grocery shop in the worst way. Cantaloupe would be nice. Genny touched her stomach as it growled in agreement.

Across the street, Harry's Hardware featured an assortment of red wagons and bicycles in the window. John hit the side of his car seat and said, "Wagon. Mine."

Catherine laughed. "He doesn't say much, but he gets his point across."

Genny grinned as she studied the sidewalk display. A bicycle could help her save on gas. She would have never thought about using one in New York. She was too afraid she'd wind up sandwiched between a couple of yellow cabs. "I might buy one of Harry's bicycles," Genny commented and adjusted her seat belt. "It's about three miles to Dr. Fleming's from my house. On nice days, I could pedal in."

Catherine shot a scrutinizing glance her way. "Suit

yourself, but have you forgotten how hot it is here in the summer? You'd be dripping with sweat by the time you met your first patient."

She had forgotten about the weather. She sure didn't want to see patients appearing as if she needed a shower. Maybe she'd wait until fall to get a bike.

Catherine pointed to the hardware store sign. "Harry isn't the name of the owner, you know."

Genny studied the bold sign above the store. "How's that?"

"His name is Alexander Steuben, but he wanted to stick with the alliteration, so he went with Harry."

Genny giggled. She was glad Dr. Fleming chose to depart from the alliterative tradition. Too bad he wasn't into flowers, though. Fleming's Florist would be perfect.

They passed the center of town and then turned around. In her mind, Genny had already spent a couple hundred dollars cruising Main Street. It's good it was in her mind and not coming out of her wallet. Della's Deli, a sandwich shop, sat on the other side of the street, and she was sure she'd be visiting, as it wasn't very far from Dr. Fleming's office. The aromas from Chen's Chinese next to Della's had her almost drooling.

After the restaurants were Ann's Antiques, Vince's Vintage, and Colleen's Collectibles, which appeared to make that part of Worthville the go-to place for antique shopping. She loved vintage items, but because of her financial situation, it'd be a while before she'd be shopping for home furnishings.

Across the street from the depot sat the old feed store. It still bore the remnants of a painted red-and-black advertisement on its brick exterior—Need Feed? Buy Mead. Her grandmother had filled her mind with stories from her childhood and how the feed store had been a place their family visited often—such an idyllic time riding into town, stopping for an ice cream at the old soda fountain in Wheaton's Drugs, which was now Connie's Coffee and Cones, and then picking up the supplies they'd need for the week at the feed store. Back in those days, the pastures behind the farmhouse she lived in were alive with cattle and horses.

The feed store appeared to be an office building now with a small sign out front. *Wait, what is the name on the sign?* She leaned forward and squinted—David Worth, Attorney at Law. Her stomach tightened. So that's where he devised his underhanded maneuvers. *Good to know.* She'd be sure to steer clear, glad he wasn't *her* attorney.

She shook off the information, determined to not let it ruin her day. Even with all the traffic, they found a parking space right in front of the depot, vacated by another minivan with a bumper sticker that read, "Proud Parent of a Worthville Wolverine." Was there no end to the alliteration obsession?

A sign on the depot appeared to have been recently restored and announced in a bold font, Worthville Train Depot. Zinnias shouted from every flowerpot, window box, and bed around the depot, and scads of people spilled from its doors. A petting zoo with pigs, chickens, and sheep occupied the depot parking lot while a clown handed out balloons.

Food vendors lined the sidewalks, selling hot dogs, cotton candy, barbecue, and Genny's personal favorite:

funnel cakes. She remembered almost getting sick from all the sugar one time when she was a kid, but it had been worth it.

Two giant blow-up slides had Lauren and John almost coming out of their car seats.

As they exited the car, Catherine held out her hand to her children. Lauren took it at first, but as they passed the sheep, she went for an endearing brown-and-white one. After protesting being dragged away, she at last gave in to her mother's instructions. "Come on, kids. Let's check out the art exhibit inside first; then we'll see the animals."

Genny thought the exhibit might be lost on the kids but followed them into the depot anyway. Thoughts about David Worth and his ill intentions kept trying to edge back into her mind, but she again determined she would not let him take this day from her. Having made that decision, she stepped into the renovated space and the heaviness lifted.

CHAPTER FOUR

G ENNY TOOK IN THE FAMILIAR YET refreshed depot. Paintings, colorful quilts of various designs, and pottery pieces on pedestals lined the walls. "I don't even know how long it's been since I've been in this building."

Catherine nodded. "I've often wished I could've seen it when the Georgia Railroad came through here. It makes a nice town hall and art gallery, though."

"I remember Grandmother talking about riding the Georgia Railroad. She loved recalling the kind engineers and porters and the *clickety-clack* of the train. She would ride to Atlanta to go shopping at the downtown Rich's, and at the end of the day, she'd take the train back home and eat dinner in the dining car."

A dreamy glaze crossed Catherine's eyes. "It sounds so wonderful. Something out of a movie."

"It does." Genny let her mind wander to what it might have been like to ride with her grandmother on the old Georgia Railroad. Genny had always had a soft spot in her heart for history and tradition. Her grandmother called her an "old soul." She guessed she was. As she rubbed a distressed timber in the depot, she spotted David Worth coming toward them, jolting her out of the past. She turned, pretended not to see him, and studied a quilt on display. *What is he doing here?* She hoped he didn't see her.

"That's a nice one, isn't it?" David asked.

She cringed and turned. "Hello, Mr. Worth," she said in her professional nurse practitioner voice.

"Good to see you again." He tipped his head toward Catherine. "And you too, Catherine."

Catherine nodded to him as Lauren pulled on her sleeve. "Mom, they have funnel cakes outside. Can we get one?"

"Genny, if you don't mind, I'm going to slip outside to get the kids a snack. I'll catch you later. David, good to see you again."

"But..." Genny tried to protest her leaving, but Catherine waved and sauntered off with her kids. She turned to David with reluctance. "You and Catherine know each other?"

"Go to the same church." David jammed his hands in his pockets.

Church? The man she'd made him out to be in her mind was incongruous with churchgoing.

David directed his blue eyes toward her. "I know this is awkward. I'm sorry we started poorly. You were right about a conflict of interest. Last night, I called Saul Lance, told him I couldn't represent him anymore and that I shouldn't have taken him on to begin with—it wasn't ethical."

Genny turned back to the quilt and thought about David's words. She hadn't seen them coming. She had to give it to him, though; he was at least trying to do the right thing. That was refreshing. She glanced at him again. Could she trust this man? The only reason she would consider trusting him was that her grandmother had done so by putting her legal matters into his hands. With Genny's past experiences, she found it easier to trust her grandmother's judgment than her own. So if Agnes Sanders trusted David, she would try to trust him too. "I'm glad to hear that."

He responded with that endearing smile she'd seen when she first met him. "Let me buy you a hot dog?"

She nodded, and David gestured outside.

When they bought their hot dogs—his chili, no onions, and mustard, hers ketchup and pickle relish—they took a seat at a picnic table while the crowd milled around them. Zinnias bloomed in a flowerpot in the center of the table. Genny took a bite of her hot dog, chewed, and swallowed. "As a kid, I used to count the days till the Zinnia Festival."

David nodded and scanned the crowd. "How does Worthville stack up against the Big Apple?" He snacked on one of his fries.

Genny chuckled inside. No one called New York that anymore, but Genny didn't say it. She joined him in surveying the scene of kids running to the petting zoo, lines of people at the food trucks, and the riot of color from the zinnias for sale. "I miss the city, but I don't yearn for fighting to get on a subway every morning, and I for sure don't ache for the cramped apartment I rented. People here have walk-in closets bigger than my apartment in New York.

"Last, but not the least of all, I love the Southern temperatures. I am not a cold weather girl. I almost froze to death in Manhattan." Genny involuntarily shivered, thinking about having to brave the single-digit temperatures in January, not to mention the snow, which turned into gross gray mounds pushed to the curb by snow plows. No, she didn't miss the weather.

"Lots of snow, huh?" he asked.

"Yes, and not in a pretty way. It's rough having to navigate through it on the way to work every morning." She turned her attention to the town around her. "I love this town, its history, and its traditions. I love that it has one foot in the past and one in the future." She regarded the depot. "And that the town fathers and mothers have taken extra trouble to preserve the past for the next generations." She then took such a large bite of her hot dog, she covered her mouth with her hand to have privacy for chewing.

David smiled and averted his eyes. "Sounds like you're here to stay."

Genny swallowed at last. "Well, like I told you, this town and my grandmother's house mean a lot to me... for many reasons."

David nodded toward the depot. "How'd you like the art exhibit?" He made the last of his hot dog disappear.

"I haven't seen it all yet, but what I did see was good. Wish I could've seen my grandmother's work exhibited in that depot. She stopped painting in her twenties, though."

David took a sip from his soda. "Why's that?"

Genny swallowed the last bite of her hot dog and plucked one of the zinnias from the pot in front of her. "Said she lost her ability to see, whatever that means. There's one painting of hers left. It hangs over the mantel."

Catherine approached David and Genny with a wave of her hand, but Lauren and John were nowhere in sight.

"Where are the kids?" Genny asked, concerned.

"I left them with my cousin at the petting zoo since they were having such a great time with the goats. Now I can go in the depot and actually enjoy the artwork."

Genny stood. "I'll join you."

David rose to his feet as well. "I have to go, but good to see you both."

Genny waved good-bye. "Thanks for the hot dog."

"My pleasure," he said with a big smile.

She guessed they'd at least somewhat mended the rift between them. David wasn't such a bad guy after all, once she pushed past the Saul Lance issue. And what was it with his smile? *Winsome* was the word that came to mind. She shook her head to clear it and followed Catherine into the depot.

Inside, they circled around the interior walls of the depot, giving attention to each of the creations displayed. They came to a striking rendering of the Worthville depot and studied it a moment. "I love this painting. The proportions are perfect," Catherine observed.

Genny scrutinized the painting and thought the pitch of the roof was a little off, but she didn't say anything. She tended to overanalyze things. She took a step back, trying to see what Catherine saw, and the overall effect was nice.

Out of nowhere, a big, burly man with a potbelly and a toothpick hanging out of his mouth lumbered alongside her.

As Genny turned to him, his eyes narrowed, which reminded her of a snake whose head she'd cut off at her grandmother's house one summer day when she was in high school.

"You Genevieve Sanders?" His booming voice made people around them turn in their direction.

"I am." This man's menacing tone made Genny's skin crawl. She wanted to run but planted her feet on the floor. She wouldn't let him bully her.

"I'm Saul Lance. My lawyer—or should I say my former lawyer?—David Worth, told me last night he couldn't represent me anymore..." He pulled the toothpick from his mouth and moved closer. "Something about a conflict of interest. What kind of spell did you drop on him?"

Genny glanced at Catherine, then back to Lance. "You'll have to talk to him about this, not me." She owed Lance no explanation. She didn't care how puffed up he became.

Lance put the toothpick back in his mouth. "I'm putting you on notice that I'm going to get that land of yours. I've spent too much time and money putting this deal together."

Genny straightened to her full five-feet, six-inch height. "Is that a threat?"

"No, it's a fact." He let go a laugh that made Genny's blood run cold and slithered away. Genny and Catherine stared at each other, disbelieving, and then Catherine shuddered. "That guy is creepy."

Genny couldn't have agreed more.

CHAPTER FIVE

G ENNY, CATHERINE, LAUREN, AND JOHN CRAMMED into Connie's Coffee and Cones and stood in a line that extended all the way out the front door. Genny raised her eyebrows at the wait. "Popular place today."

"Worth it," Catherine said as she tried to corral her children.

Genny found Connie's decor appealing. Inspirational quotes lined the walls. One read, "'Blessed are they who see beautiful things in humble places where other people see nothing.' —Camille Pissarro." Another, "Love never fails." Genny recognized it as a Scripture verse from her childhood Vacation Bible School days. She guessed patrons could eat ice cream, drink coffee, and find a little encouragement as well. After their encounter with Saul Lance a few minutes earlier, she could use some encouragement.

"Mama, I want cookies and cream," Lauren said, pointing to a huge image of an ice cream cone on the wall. "Two scoops."

"Me too," John echoed.

As they waited their turn, a senior citizen in front of them wearing a sun hat embellished with a daisy couldn't make up her mind between lemon custard and coconut. Next in line behind her, an adolescent boy wanted three scoops, one each of turtle crunch, birthday cake, and key-lime pie. Genny cringed at the boy's combination of sweet and sour. And as she thought about sour things, Lance came back to mind, a man who had put a decidedly sour twist on her move back to Worthville. She turned to Catherine. "I'm sorry you had to hear that business with Saul Lance."

Lauren and even John were almost pulling Catherine's arms off, they were so excited about the cones. Even though they had eaten hamburgers between the funnel cakes and the cones, Genny thought the ice cream treat was bound to put them on a new sugar plateau.

Catherine glanced at the children and shook her head. "Zinnia Festival happens once a year. I let them go wild for one day; then we're back to carrot sticks and lettuce wraps." She let go of Lauren's hand for a moment to fetch a tissue from her purse, and when she did, Lauren jumped so high in the air, she almost reached Catherine's height. And Catherine was not a short woman. John then wrestled his hand away from his mom's and began his jack-in-the-box routine as well. The kids were almost bouncing off the walls or, rather, the ceiling. Catherine sighed as she apparently struggled to maintain her train of thought. "What were we talking about? Oh yes, Lance. I've never seen anything like him. What's wrong with that man anyway, and how did he know who you were?"

As Catherine grabbed her children's hands, Genny tried to give her the condensed version of the story with David and his dealings with Saul Lance.

Meanwhile, John pushed his sister.

"Hey, stop it," Lauren said.

Catherine gave John an "I mean business" look and then turned to Genny. "Aren't you scared?" she asked and paused as she glanced at the kids again. "I mean of Lance, not my kids."

Genny laughed. "He doesn't scare me, but he does make me mad and more determined to keep him from getting my grandmother's house. My picture is on Dr. Fleming's website now, so he probably looked me up, then took a chance I'd be at the festival today."

As Catherine approached the counter, a woman with curly blonde hair, whose name tag read *Connie*, peered over the counter. "Oh, look who's here. Lauren and John. I've been missing you kids. You can't stay away from Miss Connie for so long."

As if by magic, Lauren and John stopped bouncing, yanking on their mom's arms, and put on the most angelic faces. They offered the sweetest smiles.

Genny couldn't believe the transformation.

Connie smiled at Catherine. "What will y'all have? You know I have the special today." Connie paused and turned her attention to the children again. "And your kids, have you ever seen anything more precious in your whole life?"

Genny studied Lauren and John. *Cherubs, both of them.*

Connie continued, "Oh my, I believe I'm going to have to give Lauren and John free ice cream today." Her eyes met Catherine's. "If you ever get tired of those kids, you call me. I'll be glad to take them on."

They paid for their cones and left the store. As they ambled down the sidewalk, Genny licked the coffee ice cream dripping along the side of her cone. "That Connie has an amazing effect on kids, doesn't she?"

Catherine made sure the kids were following behind her. Both concentrated on their cookies-and-cream cones. "I'll say. Every time we go in there, they take to her like the pied piper."

"Do you think it's because she sells ice cream?" The sugary treat had to have a big influence.

"I think she'd have that effect if she sold used tires. She has a way with kids. I think she knows the name of every kid in Worthville."

"Good to know." Genny thought that information might be useful if she ever had kids. Of course, given Genny's track record, Connie would be retired by then.

After making one more trip to the petting zoo, they piled in the car to head home. They were hardly out of the city limits before Lauren and John fell asleep. In the quiet, Genny's thoughts turned back to the situation with Lance. Considering her history, the more she thought about it, the more she was sure it was better for her to keep her distance from Lance—and from David. After what she had been through, she needed to keep her life as simple as possible. David's lack of judgment in taking Lance on as a client didn't bode well for his future decisions.

ON SUNDAY EVENING, GENNY'S cell phone rang as she finished putting what few towels she possessed on a bathroom-cabinet shelf. One good point about living in a small New York apartment—she didn't have the opportunity to accumulate very much; therefore, less to move. She plucked the phone from her pocket and didn't recognize the number. "Hello?"

"Genny, I enjoyed speaking with you at the festival yesterday. I wondered whether you might join me for dinner Tuesday night?"

What was the conflict of emotion she felt inside? A mixture of dread and something else. Was it excitement? Surely not. Probably just the caffeine from the iced tea she'd had too late in the day. "Dinner Tuesday? I don't know."

"Or another night would work if it's better for you," David said.

She closed the cabinet door, flustered. "I just remembered—I promised Catherine I'd get together with her that night. Come to think of it, I'm pretty busy all week. New job and all. You know how it is." She'd stretched the truth to the breaking point.

She held her breath as she listened to David say, "I understand."

"Some other time, then," she said, not meaning it. "Good-bye." She clicked off the phone. That conflict again as an odd mixture of relief and disappointment settled over her. It was a little weird to go out with her grandmother's lawyer anyway.

As she sat in bed a couple of hours later, she put aside the book she'd been reading —*Guide to Physical Examination and History Taking*. She was a bit nervous about beginning a new job the next day and wanted to be at the top of her game, so she decided to cover the basics again.

As she started to turn out the light on the bedside table, a photograph of herself as a child with her mother and grandmother caught her eye, taken weeks before her mother's diagnosis when Genny was ten. At the time, her mother was already having symptoms of the rare form of leukemia that would take her life.

She remembered all too well that three days after this picture was taken, her mother came home and told them the bad news.

The pain had roared like a hurricane, but in her grandmother, she found a respite.

No one could have known it would be the last picture of them together. She touched her mother's face and fell asleep with the frame clutched to her chest.

She awoke the next morning to sunlight filtering through the curtains. She rolled over and clicked on her cell phone. She read the time—7:21—and almost leaped from the bed. How could she have forgotten to set the alarm on her first day of work? She flew to the bathroom to brush her teeth, her heart pounding, and almost tripped over the bath mat in the process. She'd never make it there by 8:00.

In minutes, she wheeled into the driveway of the Victorian home Dr. Fleming had renovated for his office. She wondered whether her clothes were on right side out. She glanced down to make sure and found they were, then glanced at the rearview mirror to see whether her hair, which she had pulled back into a ponytail in this emergency situation, looked too wild. A few sprigs of strawberry blonde stuck out wildly, and she smoothed them down. The calm scene of the house's wraparound porch filled with rockers contrasted sharply with the way she felt as she hurried to the main entrance. She reassured herself at least she didn't have to be responsible for patients today. She would only be assisting until she got her bearings, Dr. Fleming had said.

When she pushed on the door that opened into what was once a butler's pantry but now held the reception desk, she relaxed a little as she found true southern hospitality. Several staff members waited for her.

Clarice, the woman who would be the nurse and assistant working with her when she went solo with patients, greeted her. "Dr. Sanders, good to see you again. We've been counting the days until you arrived." She gave Genny a big hug. "We're like family here, and we're glad you're part of it."

The young receptionist behind the counter stood and extended her hand. "I'm Maddy. So glad to meet you. I'm sorry I wasn't here when you visited before. There's never been a nurse practitioner in Worthville until now. I'm hoping to go into medicine myself, but I haven't decided which field. I'm taking classes at the university over in Perdue right now."

Genny nodded as a couple of other nurses also greeted her, and then Clarice said, "Dr. Fleming was called to the hospital on an emergency right before you arrived. He wanted me to tell you he's sorry he couldn't be here to personally welcome you back to Worthville. He should be here in a few minutes, though."

Genny nodded. Often, as a medical professional, someone else's needs determined how one spent his or her time.

The phone rang as Genny stood there, and Maddy answered. She mouthed to Genny, "Dr. Fleming." She nodded a couple of times and said, "She's standing right..." But the phone must have clicked off on the other end. "I'm sorry. He was in a huge hurry. He said he was going to be tied up a lot longer than he thought but he was confident you could handle things this morning without him."

Oh no, she thought.

CHAPTER SIX

THAT PHONE CALL THREW GENNY INTO the deep end of the pool seeing patients. What a day to be late. For a brief period of time years ago, she worked triage in an emergency room—she hoped it all came back to her. That and the job she just left in family practice. She was sure glad she reviewed the night before, as an array of ailments were bound to present themselves

Tim Lewis, an eight-year-old boy, had fallen from his bicycle, and after an X-ray, Genny found he suffered a buckle fracture in his distal radius. She referred him to an orthopedic specialist in a nearby town. He'd heal in a few weeks and wasn't too upset by the incident, until Genny told him he must stay off his bike for a month. "And school just got out," he muttered and stuck out his lower lip.

Elias Glynn, eightyish, needed a refill on his diabetes medicine. She struggled to communicate with him because of his hearing loss and ramped up the volume in her voice. "I'm changing your dosage!"

"Why do I need voltage?" Then he grinned. "I'm pretty bright already."

Genny increased the decibel level even more, though she might be violating privacy laws as the patients in the waiting room were sure to hear her. "Dosage, not voltage."

He slapped his knee. "Why didn't you say so to begin with? Postage. If you need postage, I can stop by the post office on the way home."

Genny wondered whether he was putting her on, and she sat on a stool, stumped. She glanced over at Clarice, who used her hand to mimic writing on a pad. Why hadn't she thought of that? Genny wrote out the instructions and handed them to him.

She watched as he realized what she was saying.

He said, "Got it."

She barely managed to communicate she was calling the prescription in before he made his exit. Maybe he really couldn't hear after all.

She hoped she hadn't embarrassed him. These were the kinds of challenges she'd face daily with such a diverse practice as Dr. Fleming's. How he managed all these years by himself, she would never know.

Because of the high pollen count for the past couple of weeks, many of her patients suffered from allergies, and she recommended upping their antihistamine dosage, but a couple had developed sinus infections and needed antibiotics.

With folks out in their gardens and yards more, several came in with poison ivy rashes. One lawn maintenance worker presented such a bad case, she gave him a steroid shot to cut the inflammation. She hoped the shot worked wonders. Heat made the itching worse, and with his outside job, there was no getting away from the soaring June temperatures. Genny thought about having a garden, but it was a little too late to be planting, and she was overwhelmed anyway. Maybe next year, if Al could help.

A couple of patients needed wellness exams. She was glad she found no concerns in her examinations of them.

About midday, Genny read the name *Harriet Glaussen* on the chart of her next patient. She entered the examination room, noting that the patient's age marked her as a senior citizen, so she was a little surprised when Clarice whispered, "Live wire," when they stepped through the door.

Wearing a blue hospital gown as she sat on the exam table, gray-haired Harriet said, "I've been sitting here so long, I was about to order pizza. You want yours with pepperoni or ground beef?" She grinned at Genny in a compelling way.

Clarice stifled a laugh and busied herself straightening a few magazines on a counter.

Genny tried to maintain her professional manner and extended her hand. "Mrs. Glaussen, I'm Genny Sanders, Dr. Fleming's new nurse practitioner. Glad to meet you, and sorry about the wait."

Harriet took her hand. "Call me Harriet, like Agnes did. We were friends, and she used to brag on her nurse practitioner granddaughter. I feel like I already know you. And don't worry about the wait. This was nothing compared to other days I've been here. Why, I believe I collected my first social security check while sitting in one of Dr. Fleming's waiting rooms. It's about time he got some help around here."

Genny tried not to giggle. "Glad to hear we're making progress." She scanned Harriet's chart. "So you were friends with my grandmother?"

Harriet nodded. "Sure miss her too, like I know you do."

Genny glanced away from the chart. "I wish I hadn't lived so far away so I could've visited more often. She must've been lonely."

Harriet laughed and slapped her knee. "She might've been alone, honey, but I guarantee she wasn't lonely, and she made sure no one else in her circle was either." The look in Harriet's eyes grew distant. "Agnes about saved my sanity with my husband, Homer, having Alzheimer's and all." Harriet tugged on her hospital gown, trying to make it cover more of her legs than it was meant to. "We retired here about the time you went off to school, I guess. Not long after, Homer became ill. Sometimes I'd be homebound so long, I started feeling as if I was getting the disease too. Then Agnes would appear and make me laugh again."

"Others have said she had a way of doing that." Genny flipped another page on the chart, glanced at the page, and then directed her attention back to Harriet.

"After Homer died, she stayed with me through those hard days." Harriet then gazed at Genny. "Now changing the subject. What do you know about my blood pressure?"

Genny flipped the chart back to the first page and studied it a moment more. "Well, according to the vitals Clarice took before I came in, I know we've still not found the right medicine dosage. That's why you're having erratic readings." Genny thought for a moment. "I'll need to see you more often. Once a week is best."

Harriet squirmed on the exam table. "I guess I don't have much choice."

Genny smiled. "I'll have Clarice make an appointment for next week." She handed Harriet a paper. "I know Dr. Fleming has probably already reviewed this with you, but I want to make sure you observe this diet. It's especially important you keep your salt intake low."

Harriet took the paper, glanced at it, and put it in her lap. Since Harriet hardly acknowledged the diet information, Genny reiterated her point. "That information can save your life. Please pay attention to it."

Harriet nodded. "Oh, sure. I've seen it before. Am I going to be seeing you rather than Dr. Fleming from now on?"

"If you don't mind." Genny hoped she didn't. It was going to be a rough road here in Worthville if patients didn't want her taking care of them.

Harriet raised her eyebrows. "Mind? He's become such a curmudgeon. I'd be pleased to see you instead. He was always fussing at me about one thing or another."

Genny noted Clarice trying to contain another

giggle.

Harriet eased off the exam table as Genny headed for the door.

"Oh, and Dr. Sanders?"

Genny turned around.

"You're a mighty blessed young woman. Your grandmother left you quite a legacy."

"Thank you," Genny said. "I'm going to enjoy the house."

"That's not what I was talking about," Harriet said.

Genny started to ask her what she meant, but Maddy met her in the hallway. "Dr. Sanders, Dr. Fleming has called back and says he needs to speak to you about a patient you're seeing this afternoon."

"You talk to him. I'll see you next time." Harriet waved goodbye.

Genny waved back, puzzled. She dialed Dr. Fleming, who gave her his insights on a challenging diabetic patient she would be seeing that after noon. As she clicked off the phone.

Clarice went by her and said, "I'll get the vitals and you take a little break. Give me two minutes."

Two minutes today was like a vacation. She dashed to the break room, poured a half cup of coffee, sat down, put her feet up on a chair, and took a big sip of hot caffeine. She could use extra energy.

It gave her about a minute to think about what Harriet might have meant by her grandmother leaving her a legacy. Legacy came in many shapes and sizes for sure. If Harriet wasn't talking about the house, she guessed she must be referring to her grandmother's fine character. Genny could only hope to be the kind of person her grandmother was. She certainly set the bar high. On the other hand, if folks in Worthville thought she would be involved in the community in the same way her grandmother was, she thought that an unreasonable expectation. She couldn't see herself serving on five different church committees, teaching kids' classes in Sunday school, and being in the Worthville Historical Society. That just wasn't her.

"Dr. Sanders?" Clarice slid into the room without Genny noticing.

"Are you ready for me?" Genny took another sip of coffee.

"Yes, I took Mr. Akins's vitals, and he showed me a rash." Clarice exhaled sharply and drummed her fingers on a stack of files in her hand.

"And?"

"Looks like shingles to me." Clarice switched from drumming her nails to tapping her foot, showing exasperation.

Genny stood, poured the last of her coffee into the break room sink, and turned back to Clarice. "Are you okay?"

"Mr. Akins is in pain, I know, but you didn't hear this from me. He can also be a pain. He ignores all the No Cell Phone signs. He talked on the cell phone the entire time I was in there. When one phone call ended, he dialed someone else. Plus"—she touched her nose— "the entire room smelled of garlic."

Just what Genny needed today—an annoying patient. Oh well. She needed to buck up and deal with it.

She hoped Dr. Fleming didn't mind her giving the patient an ultimatum—lose the cell phone or find another doctor. Shingles or no shingles, she wasn't putting up with it.

CHAPTER SEVEN

FTER SUCH A TIRING FIRST WEEK, Genny was glad Al couldn't get over to her house until after noon on Saturday, and she intended to sleep late. But she couldn't get something off her mind, and by eight thirty, she'd already been up an hour holding the key box in her hand, trying keys from it in various locks. The box was a jumble. Two or three keys she remembered using when she lived there, but since it was so long ago, she was clueless as to what many went to. Her grandmother was many wonderful things. Organized wasn't one of them.

She inserted a key in a closet door, but it didn't work. She took out another key and inserted it in the lock, and it turned. She put the box on a nearby chair, pulled a cardboard tag from her pocket, and looped it through the key. She wrote on the tag, "Guest room closet." From the closet, she moved to a blanket chest and tried keys. She found the correct one for the chest and labeled it as well. Then she turned on a couple of fans upstairs to fight the stifling heat due to no insulation in the house. She pulled her hair into a ponytail. It looked as if she'd have only one hairstyle this summer. She didn't know whether it was from having acclimated a little to colder weather and then coming south, but this summer felt hotter than usual.

There had been so many changes since the building of this house. No one locked their exterior doors back then, yet for a reason beyond understanding, Genny's grandfather put a lock on every closet, and much of the antique furniture also featured locks on the doors and drawers. She never remembered anybody using the keys except the ones for the outbuildings.

Genny moved into the hall, opened the closet there, and stepped back from the avalanche of boxes sliding out. Several box tops fell off and scattered across the floor. She knelt and read the black marker writing on the top of one. It read, "Receipts and IRS returns." There was no date, and the box was sealed in a haphazard way. Other boxes had no tops at all. She tried to match box lids with boxes, but some weren't labeled. *These can't be her financial records. Are they?*

Genny thought of her labeled financial files all with uniform folders in a fireproof filing cabinet. She'd placed the cabinet in the downstairs coat closet after first emptying it of old Christmas lights, which she concluded were sure to be a fire hazard. Though she kept fond memories of stringing the lights on the front porch at Christmas, she didn't want to burn the house to ashes with lights manufactured around the same time Dr. Christiaan Barnard performed the first heart transplant. She did not hesitate to toss them. If she grew nostalgic for porch lights, she'd buy newer, safer ones.

This mess was too much to deal with right now. Somehow she managed to shove the boxes back in the closet, found which key fit the lock, and then leaned against the door to close it. Genny studied the contents of the key box and said aloud, "Well, that's it. They're all labeled except this one—the one with the red ribbon."

She dangled the key in the air. "Do you go to anything at all?" She shook her head at the mystery and moved toward a nearby trash can. She held the key over the trash can, dropped it, and headed toward the stairs. When she reached the landing, she sensed a nudge inside that she should go back to get it. She tried to ignore it, but by the time she reached downstairs, the nudge was more pronounced. It seemed ridiculous, but she turned around anyway, scaled the steps two at a time, went to the trash can, retrieved the key, and returned it to the box. *Pointless clutter*, she thought. Still, it did have that red ribbon around it, almost as if her grandmother was making a point.

Catherine came over in the evening to help Genny clean out her kitchen cupboards. Genny was unprepared for the enormity of the job. They sifted through canned goods and filled half a trash bag with expired soups and rusted cans of tomatoes and other vegetables. "Ohh, look at this." Catherine held two cans of tuna. "I haven't seen this label in years."

"Must have been left over from when I lived here." Genny took the cans from her. "Agnes Sanders wouldn't touch tuna. She said two cans of tuna are what Jesus used to feed the five thousand."

Catherine burst out laughing. "Agnes was such a wit. I remember her saying tuna is so bad, two cans would feed five thousand people because nobody wanted it."

Genny had found that her grandmother took to eating out more and more over the years. She'd told Genny she bought dinner at a local restaurant, ate half of it, and then saved the other half for dinner the next night. "Cheaper than cooking myself," she'd said. Genny guessed she tired of eating alone too, because much of the food in the cabinets bore long-expired dates. Genny ached for those long-ago days when she could share meals with her mother and grandmother. She scrutinized the expiration date on a can of chili. Two years out of date. She threw it in the trash can.

"So no air-conditioning?" Catherine patted her brow with a paper towel.

"No air-conditioning. But it's not too bad in the kitchen because the oak tree out back provides good shade. Where it's bad is upstairs."

"I feel for you." Catherine moved green-bean cans to the counter to examine them.

"I'm making small improvements now, but when I get a little ahead, one of my first big projects will be to install central air." When that might be, however, she couldn't guess.

When they finished the canned goods, they started on the baking cabinet. Genny took out a box of oatmeal. "I wonder how old this is?" She opened the top and inspected the contents. "I don't remember Grandmother ever cooking oatmeal. She was more of a grits kind of woman."

The women both laughed, and Genny tossed the oatmeal in the trash. She then proceeded to check out a bag of flour, which she found still in date and free of vermin. She placed it back in the cupboard. Her grandmother's one meal exception to eating out— breakfast. When she was not on call and able to visit at Christmas, she found that her grandmother still loved to have toasted biscuits in the morning, so she'd make a pan of biscuits, refrigerate them, and toast one in the toaster oven each morning. Genny was going to miss those biscuits. Why couldn't she have learned to make them when she had a chance?

Catherine sorted through a spice rack, checking dates. "Have you recovered from that situation with Lance?" She tossed a couple of bottles in the trash, then opened a jar of parsley and sniffed. "You ought to be careful." She put the lid on the parsley and threw it away too.

"He's a bag of air." Genny pulled cornmeal out of the cabinet and opened the top. When she did, a mouse sprang from the bag. The mouse made a dash for the laundry room, and Catherine squealed. Genny had seen her share of field mice living in this farmhouse, so it was no surprise to her. Catherine moved here from the city, though, and maybe wasn't as accustomed to rodents encroaching.

Catherine hopped on a chair. "What was that?"

Genny laughed. "Welcome to country living. He was a tiny mouse." Genny stopped a moment. "Don't you have them at your house?"

"If I did, I would have already moved."

Catherine's house was newer, so Genny thought it must have been better insulated from intruders. "I'll see where he's off to."

"Make sure he's off to the outside." Catherine stood as still as a sculpture on the chair, scanning the room for the furry critter.

Genny checked around in the laundry room and at first found no way for a mouse to enter or exit the premises, but when she checked behind the dryer, there was a huge hole in the vent pipe along with what appeared to be the beginnings of a nest. "The mouse is gone," she shouted to Catherine.

"Are you sure?" Catherine asked.

"Pretty sure." Genny made a mental note of what would be the first project on Al's list for the next Saturday. She wasn't afraid of mice, but they could chew books, linens, and whatever else they could get their little gnawing teeth on. Meanwhile, she would keep the laundry room door shut to all other intruders until Al could replace the vent. She put a towel along the space under the door to make sure nothing small could get through, at least not without an effort. She didn't like mousetraps around.

Catherine stepped off the chair. "You know, I think I'm shot for the day. I'm not much on rodents, and if I were to open a box with one in it, I believe I'd test all the medical skills you have."

"I understand. Living in the country has its good points, but there are a few negative facets to deal with."

Genny was tired too and thought she might go to bed a little earlier than usual since she'd risen early to try to solve the key mystery. After all, she had meant to sleep late this morning.

After Catherine left, Genny wanted to make sure the mouse didn't get into the laundry room cabinets. One of them might have been left open. Besides, she needed to check out how much cleaning would have to be done in there. When she opened the cabinet, a couple of paintbrushes stood in a jar. She smelled the brushes. "Turpentine, pretty fresh—wonder what she used these for." Genny stepped into the kitchen and surveyed the scene around her, trying to spot anything with fresh paint. It appeared a brush hadn't touched these walls in a decade—everything was the same color as when she left home. Besides, these appeared to be artist's brushes. She shook her head as she stepped back in the laundry room and put the brushes in the cabinet.

What was the word her grandmother used to use for a mystery? Oh yes. *Enigma*. Well, this was an enigma for sure.

CHAPTER EIGHT

GENNY'S CELL PHONE RANG MIDDAY ON Sunday. *Oh no,* she thought when she saw the number. She clicked on the phone. "Hello?"

"Genny, I hope your week went well," David said.

"Pretty crazy. New job, you know." Not to mention Dr. Fleming being called away to the hospital several times, but she didn't say that.

"I hear you. Well, I know you said you were packed last week, but I wonder if you might be free this afternoon. I thought we'd go for a drive. I'd love to show you something—of historical interest, since you like that sort of thing. We could come back to town, grab a bite to eat, and then stop by Connie's for ice cream. She has a new peanut butter flavor you have to try. And if you don't want that, you can always get an iced coffee."

"Okay, that sounds fine." *Rats.* Why did she say that? How did she allow herself to get roped into going out for a drive with David? He caught her so off guard, she didn't have her excuses ready.

"See you in a few minutes, then," he said and hung up.

She put her phone back in her pocket. What excuse could she have used? She could have said she needed downtime. Quite truthful. Of course, he would have come back and said this was going to be downtime. She tried to think of another reason not to go, and for the life of her, she couldn't. She sighed and started upstairs to change. She guessed the least she could do was not wear old yoga pants.

She slipped on a sundress, buckled on a pair of sandals, and turned from side to side to study her reflection in the vanity mirror. *Not bad for last minute.* With no idea what David wanted to show her, she thought the sundress hit it right in the middle. Not too dressy. Not too casual.

Wheels ground across the crushed rock in the driveway outside. Genny gave her hair a quick brush, descended the stairs, and started toward the door. At the last minute, she decided to grab her purse. She hated to lug a handbag around, but she might need it for lip gloss or her hairbrush.

David met her at the porch steps. "You look great."

"Thanks. So where are we going?" She hadn't meant to be so direct.

David grinned. "You'll see. Hop in."

He held the passenger door open for her, something she hadn't experienced in years. In fact, she rarely rode in a car when she lived in New York. Except for cabs, of course. She never owned a vehicle because she didn't want to pay the exorbitant fee to park it in the city. She rode the subway to work—the station was just around the corner from her apartment. She bought her used SUV just before coming back to Georgia.

They headed toward town, then turned northeast and cruised toward a part of the county she hadn't been to in years. As they drove through the countryside, Genny grew quiet as she marveled again at the beauty of this part of Georgia. Fence-lined pastures surrounded old homesteads, many now long abandoned as the community moved from an agrarian society to an urban one. They left the fields of cotton and corn to get jobs in factories or offices. From the looks of the fields, not much of this land was under cultivation anymore.

Genny remembered the question she wanted to ask David. "Are you the Worth of Worthville?"

David laughed as he clicked on his left-turn signal. "Well, not me, but someone way back in my family was the Worth of Worthville. My great-great-grandfather."

"Why didn't I know any Worths as a child?" She'd tried and tried to think of someone with that surname from her childhood, but she couldn't remember even one. David made the turn, and Genny still couldn't figure out where they were headed.

"My grandfather moved away from Worthville in the forties, and my father was born in Atlanta."

"So you grew up in Atlanta?" she asked.

"I did and went to law school at Emory, but I wanted to come back here." David hit his blinker again to turn right. He wheeled the SUV onto a dirt road.

Where are we going? She lived in the country. This was the other side of nowhere.

She couldn't imagine having such a definite career destination. She'd taken the job in New York because of the great pay, but she sure missed the South and the warm weather. "How did you know that? I mean, how did you know you would come back here?"

David made another turn, finger combed his hair, and paused a moment before answering. "It's kind of a long story." He pointed to his right. "There it is."

Through the trees that lined the road, an old mill appeared in the distance—the kind with a wheel. "Is that what I think it is?"

"It's the Worth mill—the gristmill my great-great-grandfather built and operated for years. This whole community was built up around the mill." David scanned the empty landscape. "Or what used to be the community. Anyway, it's how Worthville got its name."

Genny studied the mill a moment. "Can we get closer?"

"Sure." With that, David abruptly took off across the field on what apparently used to be a dirt road. She could make out two parallel tracks now crossed by deep ruts, which made the SUV rock. They bumped over what Genny guessed was a firebreak and came to rest near the mill. She opened the door and stepped out. As she did, she could hear the rushing of a stream and moved toward the sound.

As she stood on the bank, the tumbling waters that once powered the mill coursed downstream. Though the mill was in disrepair, the waterwheel itself appeared amazingly intact. She turned to David, who had followed her. "This is incredible. Who does it belong to?"

"Me." David grinned. "Somehow I was bequeathed it in all the property dispersals over the years." He lowered his voice and turned to her as if to divulge some secret. "I don't think anybody else in the family wanted it, so that's why they gave it to me." He gazed at the mill with admiration. "You know, I've thought about living out here. It's so peaceful. My great-great-grandfather began the feed store in town as well, but the property has changed hands several times through the years. Fortunately, I was able to buy it when I moved back here."

Genny was impressed by David's commitment to family history. Not many people their age cared about roots. Genny turned to the mill again, imagining the wheel turning and wagons rolling along the road to deliver their crops. She wished her grandmother was around so she could ask her about it. "Why didn't I know this was out here?"

"It used to be a local landmark, but over the years, as the old folks died and new people moved in, I guess everyone forgot about it." Once more, David turned his head and considered the surrounding countryside. "It's not like it's on the way to anywhere."

True. But still. There might be an interest in it if it were to be renovated. "Did you hear stories about it from your family?"

"Not from my dad, that's for sure. But I was in the attic one day when I was in high school, and I found a box of letters from my great-grandfather to my grandfather when he was in military service. He talked about the mill his dad started, which at the time he was running, and the customers, and..." He paused a moment as if checking to see if she were interested.

Genny couldn't wait to hear what was next. "And...?"

"I guess I was hooked. I wondered whether the mill itself was still standing. I asked my dad, but he didn't know. It's as if this place never existed to him." David frowned. "Over the years, he became more and more consumed with that Atlanta lifestyle." David stepped a few feet closer to the mill. "And this is a long way from Buckhead." He sighed.

Genny was familiar with that part of Atlanta. Very upscale. One of the richest zip codes in the country.

David continued, "When my grandfather left the property to me in a trust, my dad expressed no interest in it." He shook his head. "In fact, he said, 'Who would want an old run-down place like this in the middle of nowhere?'"

Genny stepped beside David. "Can we peek inside?"

David took her hand, and she was surprised at how comfortable it felt. Together, they waded through the overgrown grass surrounding the mill. David pushed open a door fashioned of primitive boards nailed together and stepped over a threshold. The interior of the mill boasted what she thought might be heart-pine floors, still in good condition. Even through the accumulated dust, the deep grain of the wood shone.

David held an arm in front of her as she made a move to go forward. "We'd better not go much further.

The floors look to be in good condition, but you never know when one might give way. I need to get an engineer out here to check the building's structural integrity."

Genny touched one of the supporting timbers and tried to understand some of the milling machinery which lay covered in dirt and cobwebs. "What did they do here?"

"It was used to grind corn into grits and cornmeal. Don't you wish we could have a taste of what came from this mill?"

Genny grew up eating grits, and if there was one thing she missed the most in the past few years, it would be cheese grits for breakfast. She directed her gaze to David. "I think you should renovate."

"Maybe, sometime. It'd take quite a bit of money to do it. I've been saving." A flicker of doubt surfaced in his eyes.

"I think folks would consider it worth the drive out here. There's not a place like it anywhere around." Genny could see families with children coming out to see the way life used to be, to find a place of solace in a world of soccer games, dance lessons, and running from one thing to another. The older generation would be enthralled by the slice of history this mill represented.

David raised his eyebrows at the suggestion and came across as unconvinced. "It's a dream."

Genny studied the cobweb-and-dirt-covered gears and shafts of the mill. "How did it work?"

David raised his eyebrows at her and laughed. "You're asking me?"

She scanned the area around them. "I don't see anyone else." If she were a betting woman, she'd guess he'd already researched the topic.

He took a deep breath. "I'm in no way an expert." He pointed to a big gear. "The waterwheel outside turned that gear there, which I believe is called a pit wheel. It turned a gear on that vertical shaft." He moved his finger, gesturing to a large pole. "And of course, the top millstone, called a runner, is on that shaft. It was adjusted in its proximity to the bottom millstone depending on the fineness of the grain. There's a few more details that I've forgotten, but those are the basics."

"Good explanation. I get it."

They stood a moment longer, taking in the workings of the mill, and then he took her arm and guided her back through the door toward the car. They sat in the vehicle under the canopy of giant oaks that surrounded the mill. Genny hit the switch on the window, and a slight breeze blew through. She took in a deep breath, expanding her lungs. "So nice out here." She was glad she'd come. "Thank you for inviting me." Here she was in the middle of nowhere with this man she hardly knew, yet it was as if they'd known each other for years. As she shifted in her seat, she let her hand touch his arm, and a slight charge jolted her from her placid state. What was it with this man?

David placed his hand on hers and nodded. "You are quite welcome. I thought maybe you'd appreciate the mill." He lingered a moment in that position, but then awkwardness encroached. He cranked the car and put it in reverse. "I'm hungry. Let's go to Della's."

With no food since breakfast, she welcomed the suggestion. "Great."

"And then we'll hit Connie's."

Genny's stomach was already growling. "Sounds good." Though she had already tried a couple of different sandwiches from Della's, Clarice had ordered the tuna melt the other day, and it looked delicious. She might order that.

David pressed the gas to back up.

But nothing happened except a spinning sound coming from the rear right wheel.

CHAPTER NINE

"I**SN'T THIS VEHICLE FOUR-WHEEL DRIVE?**" Genny asked.

"Two-wheel. And it appears a wheel can't get traction." He exited the car to inspect the situation. The grim expression on his face said circumstances weren't good. He returned to the car. "The axle is resting on the ground and the wheel must be spinning in the rut when I press the gas. I'm going to look around and see if I can find a board to put under the wheel. Maybe we can get traction that way."

David kicked the grass around the mill. He pulled an old board from the ground and brought it over to the car. He squatted, tinkered with the board a few minutes, and then climbed behind the wheel again. When he pressed the gas—the same sickening spinning as before. David put the car in neutral and went to the back of the car and pushed. All that happened was a little jiggling.

Genny exited the car and joined him.

"I can't let you do this," David said, his face flushed.

"I've done it before," Genny declared. On a long weekend in the Adirondacks, Genny and some friends became stuck. It took three of them, but they freed the car at last.

So on the count of three, they both gave the car a shove, but nothing happened. A little more jiggling. They tried it again. Nothing. David exhaled and turned to Genny. "I don't think we can get it out by ourselves. We're going to need a tow."

Genny reached in the car, pulled her wallet out, and slid a plastic card from its pocket. Oh, how glad she was she'd brought her purse. "I have roadside assistance. I have the number right here." She retrieved her phone, but it showed zero bars. "You don't have cell phone service out here?"

"It's one of the reasons I hesitated to live at the mill. My cell phone didn't work, and with a landline, I wasn't sure how cumbersome living here would be with clients. You know, them not being able to reach me coming and going from this place."

Genny scanned what a few minutes ago came across as enchanting countryside. Her perspective shifted. It struck her as a little desolate. "So what are we going to do?"

"I guess we'll walk."

Genny took stock of her low-heeled sandals. "I don't have shoes for walking."

David shut the car door. "If you want, you can stay here, and I'll walk."

Acres and acres of uninhabited land. No way was she staying out here in the middle of nowhere by herself.

"Walk it is." She put her roadside assistance card back in her wallet and moved to close the passenger side door.

They set out down the old dirt road. Plowing through the knee-high grass in heels, even small ones, proved quite a feat. Plus, with bare legs, briars and brush left pricks and scratches. She stopped to peel a green weed off her dress. One of the briars stuck her hand. She kept her "Ouch!" inside, not wanting to be thought of as weak. The road stretched much longer than it had when they came in. Where was the main road? A shaker-like sound near her made her freeze. "Was that a snake rattle?" She grabbed David's arm and held on, not caring anymore about what he thought.

David put his hand on hers and stopped. "I don't hear anything."

If there was a critter in the world Genny detested, it was snakes. She listened again. She'd never seen a rattlesnake in Worthville, but others in the area found them. It'd be hard to see a snake in this sea of grass. She hoped the earlier noise was a product of her imagination. She continued to hold on until they met the paved road and headed south.

They clomped along for a while, but after a few minutes, Genny stopped and removed a rock from between her sandal and her foot. Several scratches on her legs dripped blood. "You don't remember where the closest house is?" Oh, how she hoped David would say "A few more minutes."

Instead, it was "Sorry. I don't." Perspiration poured down David's face, and Genny would bet he could wring water out of his shirt. It was the hottest part of the afternoon. The scratches on her legs drew his attention, and he closed his eyes and shook his head. "I'm so sorry, Genny." He reached in a back pocket and took out a handkerchief. "It's clean."

She took it, and they stopped walking while she dabbed at the scratches. When was the last time she met a man with a handkerchief in his back pocket? It was a small comfort in the middle of the mess they found themselves in. She studied the scratches, which were going to need antibiotic ointment. She hoped she didn't brush against any poison ivy.

On top of everything else, she'd forgotten to put her sunglasses in her purse. Her stomach moved from growling to groaning at their abandoned plans. Wow, was she thirsty. She stopped again and rummaged in her handbag. She pulled out a tin and offered it to David. "Mint?

He declined, but she popped one into her mouth. At least the sundress was cool, but then her arms were turning red. Her light skin didn't take sun too well. All in all, a disastrous day. Did she not tell herself to keep her distance from David?

She almost tripped, and David tried to steady her but didn't say a word otherwise. A little compassion for him welled in her. Of course he didn't plan this, and maybe his sweaty face was red for more than one reason—maybe embarrassment.

What was wrong with her?

She should be mad, but every time she glanced at him, she could tell he was beside himself. What could she say to make the situation better? She wished she could think of something funny, but she thought she might be so near to having a heatstroke, she'd come off a little wacky. Then it came to her. "So, tell me more about the old feed store."

"Glad to." The tension in David's face eased. The worry lines on his brow faded a bit as he spoke about something other than their dilemma. "As I said, it used to house the town's feed store, which you can deduce from the sign still on the side of the building. I'm glad the renovators left it because it's part of the town's history. The building has been through many iterations but recently redeveloped into three office units downstairs and two loft apartments upstairs." He stopped to wipe his brow with his sleeve. "I bought the building, took a small office unit, just two rooms, and I live in the loft apartment upstairs. I rent out everything else."

"Oh" is all she managed to say. Her mind went blank. There was nothing to do but keep walking and keep checking to see whether bars came up on her phone.

She would have thought on a Sunday afternoon folks would be out enjoying the day, but no, they didn't see a single car. After two hours, they spotted a house where a man in overalls mowed his grass. When they trudged into the yard, he threw up a straw hat, cut the mower engine, and laughed. "You folks are having a lot of fun."

Genny tried to imagine the sight they were. David, clothes wet from perspiration, her in her cute sundress with red arms and scratched legs, not to mention the mess her hair must be.

David never smiled. "Loads of fun. You wouldn't have a phone we could use, would you?"

The man pulled a cell phone from his pocket and handed it to David.

Genny protested. "A cell phone won't work. We don't have any bars."

The man laughed again. "You have the wrong carrier. Where are you from anyway?"

Right about then, she might as well have been from Mars.

It took two hours to find a towing company to come out on a Sunday afternoon, pull them from the rut, and return home. By then, it was late.

"We could still have dinner," David said.

His statement sounded almost like a question. He had to know what she was going to say. She scanned her appearance. "I think I'll grab a sandwich at home. I'd hate to scare folks in the restaurant."

"You still look great to me."

"I think you're suffering from the heat, but no thanks." There was no way she was showing up at a restaurant appearing as if she had been on the Lewis and Clark expedition.

The only way things could have been worse that afternoon was if the man on the mower hadn't been at home. They might have walked for many more hours.

When he dropped her off at her home, David said, "Sorry it turned out this way." His head was down as he held the door for her to exit the car. He didn't say anything about seeing her again, which was fine with her. Again, he probably knew what her response would be. She resolved once more to distance herself from David Worth.

SHE NEVER CEASED TO be amazed at the range of ailments Dr. Fleming—and now she—dealt with. It was the time of year for swimmer's ear, and eight-year-old twins Chris and Craig Sebring came in with it first thing Monday morning.

A minor but painful ailment. They sat with tears streaming down their red faces, clutching stuffed animals. Chris held on to a penguin, and Craig nuzzled a dolphin. "They've been like this since yesterday," their mother said. "I can't seem to do anything that helps."

Genny's heart went out to her. Feeling helpless was a bad place to be. She doled out prescriptions for otic solutions and told them to wear earplugs in the future when taking a dip.

"Earplugs," they chorused. They became so excited over the novelty of wearing them that their tears dried up.

Tim Heston, a Worthville city worker, had a rash all over his upper body.

"Have you eaten seafood lately?" Genny asked.

"Shrimp last night," he said.

She didn't know for sure whether it was the shrimp, so she prescribed an antihistamine. "I hate to tell you this, but I must. If it is the shrimp and you eat it again, there is a danger of anaphylactic shock the next time you eat shellfish."

"I never have liked shrimp much anyway," he said. "Not worth it."

She almost needed to send Talia Meadows to the hospital. She'd been outside in the sun for two days planting a perennial border in her backyard. Her mucous membranes were dry, her urine was dark, and her pulse was rapid. "Have you been hydrating?" Genny asked.

Talia slouched on the exam table. "I don't like water, so I drink sweet tea."

"Because it's wet doesn't mean it hydrates. You need to drink water or 50 percent water, 50 percent Gatorade solution." Genny wouldn't let her go until she'd seen her down thirty-two ounces of water. In the end, Genny sent her home, with a promise from Talia she'd stay out of the sun and drink only water for a couple of days.

"Never am going to get those rosebushes in the ground," Talia mumbled.

Those were the patients she'd seen in the first hour of the day.

She began to understand why Dr. Fleming hired her. How he'd kept the ship afloat for the past few years, she didn't know. For a small town, his caseload was almost unmanageable because his excellent reputation reached far. Patients traveled from several counties all around Worthville, and he was so beloved, many patients were reluctant to allow Genny to step in for him, but so far, most complied. She managed, but barely.

It had been a Monday for sure. It didn't help she'd experienced her unfortunate excursion with David the day before. The doctor took Monday off to play golf. "First time in two years," he'd said as he headed out the door with his clubs. She was forced to take up the slack. Her feet hurt from the trek she'd been on the day before. Her skin ached from the sunburn. As she walked toward her car, she wondered whether she'd eaten lunch. She remembered half of a turkey sandwich someone brought her. Two days straight she missed meals. What a whirlwind.

As soon as her rear hit the car seat to go home, she decompressed. She wasn't sure she'd taken a deep breath all day, so she breathed in through her nose, held it for a few seconds, and let the air escape through her mouth. Oxygen. What a wonderful thing. She was going to go home and take a long bath.

Genny cranked the car and turned toward the country. When she arrived, she pulled her SUV into the usual spot behind her grandmother's car. What was she going to do with it? She didn't want the car to sit out here and rust away. She gathered the mail she had plucked from the box at the road and went inside. All she wanted to do was soak her body in a cool bath and relax. She put her purse on a table and shuffled through the mail before going upstairs, but one envelope caught her attention, and she stopped to examine it. Her brow furrowed in confusion as she read the return address and opened the letter. Her mouth went dry and her hands began to shake as she read. Confusion turned to shock at the word *foreclosure*.

CHAPTER TEN

SHE FOUND HERSELF ASKING THE SAME old question.
Did she not decide she would keep her distance
from David?

First, she said yes to what turned out to be an epic
hike and here she was entering his reception area to see
him. Seeking him out, no less. She was beginning to
question her resolve, but he was the one lawyer in town,
and though he'd been out of town yesterday, he'd
squeezed her into his schedule during her lunch hour on
Wednesday.

He insisted he would be seeing her as a friend and
not a professional. He said since they'd sort of been out
on a date already, he needed to avoid any sort of ethics
issues with dating a client. This was a fine time for him
to be thinking about ethics, given his history with Saul
Lance. Anyway, he said he couldn't and wouldn't
charge her.

She sat there feeling as if she'd been dropped
between those millstones David told her about on

Sunday, like a heavy weight was grinding away at her. This must be a mistake. She tried to breathe as she scanned the office interior. It possessed a sort of industrial feel—brick interior walls with exposed heating-and-air ducts. A nice renovation for sure. The older administrative assistant who'd asked her to be seated contrasted with the more modern aesthetic of the office.

"Could I get you coffee?" she asked from behind her desk.

"No, thank you." Genny thought for sure David would have a much younger assistant. Most of the young doctors she met got rid of their older staff because they wanted to project an up-to-date image for their patients. She assumed this young lawyer, David, would be the same way. This woman's hair was almost totally gray, and her dress was professional but old school with her nineties-style jacket and serviceable heels.

"You're Agnes's granddaughter, aren't you?"

Genny shifted in her seat. "Yes, I am."

The woman gave a big smile. "We were on a committee or two together here in town. She was a joy. You resemble her."

Genny was glad for any comparison to her grandmother, who held on to a certain beauty even into her old age.

The woman rose, moved to where Genny was sitting, and extended her hand. "I'm Louvene Walden. Nice to see you again."

Genny took Louvene's hand. "Oh, of course. I'm so

sorry. I've been gone for about ten years and haven't been back much except for brief visits." She remembered her from attending church with her grandmother.

"Honey, don't you worry about it. My wrinkles have caught up with me. I look in the mirror sometimes and say, 'Grandma, is that you?'" They both laughed, and Louvene leaned over and said in a conspiratorial way, "I told him he ought not to have gotten tangled with Saul Lance. We didn't have a clue who he was, and Agnes Sanders was a pillar in this community—the founder of the Worthville Garden Club and taught Sunday school for I don't know how long. I told him he needed to make this right."

David's door opened and an older man in a houndstooth jacket exited. "Don't forget the deposition next Wednesday," David called after him.

Louvene took on a supervisory air and directed her gaze to David. "Genny's been waiting ten minutes." Her tone held a touch of reprimand.

Nevertheless, David flashed a smile as Genny rose, and her eyes met his. For a tiny moment, something stirred inside her. Why was that? So far, David had tried to steal her house and kill her in the wilderness.

"I apologize for the wait." David gestured for her to enter his office. Patients often grew annoyed with her because of having to wait, so for a change, it was nice to be the one waiting as opposed to the other way around.

She took a seat opposite him in a leather chair. "It was nice seeing Mrs. Walden again."

"Yes, Louvene was Mr. Edward's administrative assistant for twenty-five years when he had his office in his house. When I bought the practice from him, she stayed on and came here with me." He sighed. "Sometimes I don't know whether she's my executive assistant or my mother. A bit bossy."

Genny giggled despite her dilemma.

David extended his hand. "You said you had a letter."

Looked as if he'd put on his lawyer hat, so Genny assumed the role of the client now and without a word extended the correspondence she received. He took it, and she tried not to fret as he studied the letter. Then he directed his gaze toward her. "So Lance is trying to foreclose on your house. Strange."

"The house is paid for. How can he do this?" Genny demanded. She scrutinized David while waiting on him to answer. A thought came to her. David already betrayed her trust one time. She narrowed her eyes. "Did you know about this?"

David appeared surprised, shook his head, and stammered. "What, me? No, I don't know how he did it."

Genny continued to study him. "Are you sure you're on my side?"

David nodded. "Yes, and since I cut ties with Lance, I have a poorer financial statement to prove it."

Genny relaxed a little and leaned back in her chair. "So what can we do about it?"

David dropped the letter to his desk and ran his hand through his hair—a mannerism indicating he was giving thought to a situation—a trait Genny found, in a strange sort of way, endearing.

"I can't speak to this; I'll have to research to see what's going on, but I'll get on it right away."

Genny sighed. "Let me know what you find out." She stood, and David followed suit. She'd forgotten in the South gentlemen rose from their chairs out of consideration for a woman.

David extended his hand. "I'll speak to you soon."

Genny took his hand, nodded, and left. Here she was entangled again with David Worth.

She left the building, turned left, power walked to Main Street, and went in Connie's Coffee and Cones. She didn't have time for lunch after seeing David, so she'd grab a coffee and get back to work. When she went in, she was surprised to hear Connie call out, "Dr. Sanders, it's so good to see you." Even though she spent such a long time earning her doctorate in nursing practice, it still took her by surprise when people called her by her professional title. *How did Connie remember my name with all the customers coming and going?*

"I'm doing fine." She wasn't fine at all, though. This business with the foreclosure rattled her in a way she hadn't experienced since Kurt left and her grandmother died.

Connie extended her hand and patted Genny's as it rested on the counter. "You tell me what you want. You spend all your time making folks feel better, so we're going to find something to make you feel better today."

Genny sputtered. "Decaf vanilla latte."

"Coming right up." Connie turned and busied herself preparing the latte. "How did you know you wanted to go into the medical field?"

"When I was a child and my mother was ill, I wanted to become a doctor so I could grow up and fix the horrible leukemia she suffered from. But in time, I figured out nurses made such a difference for the patients. Nurse practitioners in particular were the ones who never stood by the door with a chart in their hands, ready to leap out to the next patient, but they sat and listened. That's what set the course for my life."

Connie put her latte on the counter. "I'm sure you are making a difference in your patients' lives."

"I hope so." Genny paid.

When Connie took the money, she said, "Why don't you have a seat a minute before you dash off? It'll help you get your bearings."

Again, Genny didn't know how Connie understood her bewilderment. Did it show on her face? Over the years, Genny worked on keeping her emotions close to the vest. Instead of flying out the door as she'd planned, she took Connie's advice and sank into a seat under a plaque that bore a quote from Laura Ingalls Wilder: "It is still best to be honest and truthful; to make the most of what we have; to be happy with simple pleasures and to be cheerful and have courage when things go wrong."

She told herself, *Have courage.* She desperately hoped David would find a way out of whatever was happening. She took a sip of the latte and let the creamy liquid slide down her throat. For a few moments, in a place her New York counterparts might have considered somewhat corny, she found surprising consolation.

Corny was growing on her.

She picked up her cell phone and saw she had a

message. Her phone had been on silent all morning and she failed to move it off during lunch. The call was from David. "Hi, Genny. I went straight over to the courthouse after I saw you. It didn't take me long to find out a few things. I'm going to dig a little more before I head back to the office. I'm busy all afternoon and tonight, but I can come by your office tomorrow during lunch, if that's okay. Let me know. All right. See you then, I hope."

Wow, that was lightning-fast service. He must have shot out the door the minute she left.

She called back and confirmed the appointment for noon the next day. Maybe even after all that had happened, David Worth was going to save the day.

CHAPTER ELEVEN

O N THURSDAY, GENNY OPENED THE DOOR of her office for David, and he took a seat in the chair vacated by Mrs. Dawson, a woman who worked at a local department store and said she'd fitted Genny's grandmother for foundation garments for twenty years. She was suffering from arthritis and searching for relief. "I have to be at the top of my game for my customers," she'd said. "I'm a professional. They won't trust their fittings to anybody, you know."

Genny never felt the need to be fitted for foundation garments, as her more athletic build did not require such care. Her well-endowed grandmother did, however, and Mrs. Dawson was always a big help. Genny hoped the anti-inflammatory medication she prescribed would help her pain be more manageable. One of the biggest rewards Genny experienced as a nurse practitioner was how she helped people find a new normal, no matter what their job or position in life. When faced with health issues, almost everyone struggled to get back to regular life.

Everyone in Worthville appeared to have a relationship with her grandmother, which made Genny feel connected to her patients in a way she didn't experience at her previous job.

David kept rolling and unrolling a piece of paper in his hands, the crackling noise calling her back to the present. He exhaled a time or two in an exaggerated way. Why was he so fidgety? For a moment, she pushed her medical practice out of her mind and focused on David.

She sat opposite him. "Did you find out anything?" *Might as well get straight to the point.*

David took a deep breath. "Your grandfather borrowed $20,000 from a man named Jake Boyle back in the eighties. He used the house as collateral. Do you have any idea why?"

Genny shook her head. "I was just born, so I have no idea why he'd borrow money. He died when I was young. Grandmother never mentioned anyone named Jake Boyle." Genny took a stethoscope from her neck and placed it on the desk in front of her.

"I found the date your grandfather died in the records I was searching. Jake and your grandfather died within six months of each other. You wouldn't have known him or his heirs, because the entire family moved away not long after Jake's death. I guess Jake's heirs didn't know about the debt either."

All this mystery would have made for a great story, if she wasn't sitting in the middle of it growing more claustrophobic by the moment. She didn't have asthma, but her airways constricted. She put a hand to her throat. How would she ever find a way out of this? "Since Grandmother Agnes never mentioned it, maybe Grandfather didn't tell her." Her grandparents maintained the more typical arrangement for people of their generation. From what she understood, when her grandfather was alive, he handled the finances, and her grandmother handled affairs regarding the household and childcare. It was difficult to imagine her grandmother in such a role, as she always held the threads of their lives together in a strong way.

"The house hasn't been on the market, so..." David's voice trailed off.

Genny sat back in her chair, the words sinking in. "No one's checked the title." Genny turned toward the window in her office and gazed out in the direction of her grandmother's house, past the crepe myrtles, beyond the abelia hedge. "Grandmother never even thought about living anywhere else, never considered selling the house." She turned back to David. "So Lance did this how?"

David waved the paper in the air for emphasis. "Lance dug around and found an old security deed at the courthouse with an outstanding debt."

Genny leaned toward David, anxious to hear. "And?"

"He purchased the debt from Boyle's daughter. Though she moved away years ago, somehow Lance found her."

Genny's jaw dropped, and she gasped. "$20,000 gives him the right to foreclose on my house?"

"It does, but no problem. All you have to do is come up with the $20,000."

Genny leaned back in her chair again. The weight of reality descended, and her shoulders drooped under the load. What was she going to do?

"I never anticipated Lance would stoop so low." David shook his head and then smiled. "But at least there's an easy fix."

Genny shook her head, a cloud of defeat threatening to unload a lashing rain on her. "No, there's not." David couldn't have guessed the enormity of her situation.

"You have a good job," David said as if trying to convince her. "Even if you don't have the cash accessible, any banker would…"

She sat straight in her chair, despair giving way to determination. "I can't borrow the money, but I have to fight this foreclosure. The house is all I have." She fixed her gaze on David. She was sure he wondered why an educated nurse practitioner, who likely made good money practicing in New York City, couldn't come up with twenty thousand dollars. He had no idea what she was dealing with. "Would you talk to Lance?"

David scratched his head. "We didn't part on good terms."

"Well, you still have a relationship with him." He owed her at least this much.

He nodded with what appeared to be reluctance and placed the rolled paper on her desk. "Here's all the information. I'll let you know what Lance says."

Genny watched him go. How did things get so complicated? She put her stethoscope back around her neck, grabbed a chart from her desk, and headed out to see her next patient.

When Genny left work at an unusually early five thirty that evening, the Open sign glowed at the bookstore. She didn't have any book in mind to buy, but browsing would be nice, maybe take her mind off the foreclosure business. Who could know what treasure you might find at a bookstore? So she turned right and found a parking spot.

She opened the door to the store, and a thundering voice said, "Welcome to Tucker's Tomes." It sounded as if God were speaking to her. She glanced around and spotted a man behind the checkout counter—African American with graying hair. As their eyes met, he said, "I'm Tucker. Take your time browsing. I don't close until eight today."

Wow, Tucker could make some money doing voice-overs. Genny thought he might be able to read the dictionary and move a crowd to tears.

She browsed the local-author section, the Georgia history section, and then moved on to her favorite, biographies. Tucker chatted with customers, his voice providing a comforting soundtrack. After Genny spent a while scanning through the biographies, she selected one about Ben Carson she'd been meaning to read. She found a soft armchair and settled in. Every time the door opened, Tucker would sound his booming greeting, and for a time, the world of foreclosures and financial disaster receded. Books provided a retreat for her. She imagined she inherited the trait from her grandmother.

In what seemed like minutes, she found she'd been

there two hours. She needed to get home. As she placed the book back on the shelf and scurried to the door, Tucker called after her, "Come back soon." She hated not to buy the book, but she needed to watch every penny. One day, when circumstances changed, the first thing she would do would be to buy books.

Before bed, Genny took a moment to sit on the porch swing beside Elizabeth, who was roosting on one of the cushions. There'd be eggs in the morning for sure. Crickets chirped, and an owl hooted somewhere close by. Tree frogs joined the chorus. Even though the temperature that day had neared ninety degrees, a breeze blew across the porch, carrying the scent of jasmine, which grew on the side of the house. The sounds and smells of a thousand nights spent in the safety of this house brought comfort in the middle of all the swirling questions.

She imagined her grandmother coming to the screen door and calling for her, asking whether she wanted a snack before bed, maybe a biscuit with honey and milk. They'd bring the snack back out onto the porch and sit and talk over their day. Right about then was when Genny would have said, "Grandmother, what am I going to do about all this mess?"

Maybe her grandmother would have paused, lifted her eyes to the southern sky, and said, "I don't know, sweetie, but don't the stars look especially bright tonight?"

ON SATURDAY AL WAS already at work mowing the backyard when a knock sounded on Genny's door. "Anybody home?" David called.

Genny went to the door just as Elizabeth scurried across the porch after an insect.

She had on jeans and an NYU T-shirt and didn't look very professional. Oh well. "Come in." She unlatched the screen, held it open, and motioned for him to be seated.

David pointed to the new screen hinge. "I see you got it repaired."

"Al's a wonder. There isn't a problem he can't fix." Almost. Genny dropped into a chair. If only Al and his screwdriver could fix this mess. She tried to keep from appearing apprehensive, but she couldn't help jiggling her knee.

David steadied his gaze on her. "Lance is not budging, but it doesn't matter—I've already decided to give you the money."

Genny stood. "Give me the money? No way!"

David remained seated. "I'd rather give this money to you than get the miniscule return it's getting. It's not a loan. It's a gift."

"Listen, you were saving money to renovate the gristmill, and that's what you should do. Besides, I don't know you, so there's no way I'm taking money from you. Even if we'd been friends for years, I still wouldn't accept money. This is unacceptable." She didn't need or want his pity.

"Unacceptable?" He spread his hands in front of him. "I owe you for all this Saul Lance mess. Maybe if I hadn't gotten involved with him, this wouldn't be happening."

Genny folded her arms and shook her head. "No."

"Okay, if you won't take a gift, then take it as a loan. You can pay me back on your terms."

Unmoved, Genny said, "Renovate the mill. It's your dream. I won't take this money from you."

"If the house winds up being sold on the courthouse steps, I'll buy it; then you can pay me back."

Genny locked her arms against her body even more tightly and shook her head.

David fell back against the sofa. "But what about your dream? What will you do?"

Her resolve strengthened as she steadied her gaze on him. "I'll find a way."

"What about selling something? There must be some way to raise the cash. I've seen people raise funds online from the sale of items they didn't care about anymore."

Genny motioned around the old home. "There's nothing to sell. All I have are a few antiques Grandmother left. None would bring much."

David scanned his surroundings. "My mother was into antiques, and I learned a little from her whether I wanted to or not while accompanying her to antique stores when I was living at home."

David stood and passed a turn-of-the-century oak washstand, but Genny knew it wasn't special, except to her. He glanced at an oak table behind the sofa, refinished, again somewhat run of the mill. He peered around to the dining room table, which boasted a set of mismatched chairs to accompany the well-used drop-leaf table. It was nice, but it wouldn't bring much. Then his gaze locked on the painting above the mantel. "This offers a unique perspective on rural Georgia. The use of color is striking."

"I'm not selling the only painting of Grandmother's I have left." Her body stiffened. Again. Then she relaxed a little. "Besides, it wouldn't bring nearly enough to make a difference."

Al rode up to the house on his mower, and through the screen door, she could see him take off his hat and mop his brow. He cut the engine and stomped onto the porch.

Genny went to the door, and Al handed her a key. "I'll try to get another shed key made for you at Harry's Hardware," she said.

Al nodded. "Picking up Lori. We're going for ice cream at Connie's cause she got straight As on her end-of-the-year report card." He turned, stepped off the porch, and started wiping down his lawn mower again.

"Have you ever seen anything like it?" David peered through the window. "Does he always clean it like that?"

"He does. I thought it was a brand-new lawn mower, but Al says it's five years old."

"Most people don't treat their cars as well. Not a speck of rust on it, I'm sure."

Genny put the shed key back in the box.

"Interesting box. Appears to be hand carved." David moved beside her.

Genny caressed the box with love. "This box makes me think of my grandmother more than about anything in this house."

"Why?"

Genny grew wistful. "She said this box is like our heart, and God has placed all the keys in our heart we need to have a fruitful life, if we'll use them."

"Interesting concept. Like?"

"Like the key of love or of mercy or... you get the picture."

David nodded. "I wish I could find a solution that offered you mercy in this situation. Every piece of information I uncover bears a negative message."

Genny looked around and sighed. Sometimes she still found herself thinking her grandmother might walk in any moment.

"Does your grandmother have any financial records? Maybe we can find a document which proves she or your grandfather paid off the debt."

"Maybe. I came across papers when I was checking to see which keys fit which locks. Although"—she hesitated—"they might not be in such great order."

"Messy paperwork is no problem. Bring them to the office, and we'll scan through them. I have an appointment—I'd better get back to the office." He pivoted and faced the door.

He exited the house, stopped on the porch, then spun around and flew back. At the same time, she had an idea too. Genny arrived at the door and they shouted in unison, "The car!"

CHAPTER TWELVE

O N MONDAY, GENNY SAT PEERING AT her grandmother's car through a plate-glass window of the local used dealership aptly named in Worthville tradition Mellon's Motors. She leaned back in her vinyl-covered chair and waited for Billy Mellon, sitting opposite her, to finish his tally. Billy's slicked-back hair and Mellon's Motors embroidered golf shirt in electric blue made him every bit the stereotypical salesman.

Billy licked his pencil, jotted numbers on a spiral-bound notepad, and shook his head. "I took off for damage to the upholstery in the back seat. What did your grandmother carry around back there anyway? Looks like chicken scratches on the leather upholstery." He laughed. "Can you imagine somebody carrying a chicken around in a luxury car?" He chortled, and a big smile crossed his face at the absurdity of the idea as he again put pencil to paper.

Genny would've liked to see his face if he found out

the truth. However, she didn't go into it, thinking it might detract even further from the value if Billy Mellon learned of her grandmother's Sunday afternoon joyrides with live poultry in the back seat.

"And I couldn't give you any credit for the navigation system. It's outdated. In addition, when I drove it, it sounds like it's going to need a new transmission. It's shifting real rough." He licked his pencil again, and Genny could see he subtracted from the original figure. "So here's the final estimate."

He handed her the pad. As Genny read the number, her heart sank. She looked at him. A low four-figure offer. She expected more. "This is it?"

"Well, ma'am. It's an old car. A nice old car, but still, it won't bring much on a resale. My great-aunt owned a car like that. Ran like a top, but folks today are not looking for these big cars. If they're going to use gas, they want an SUV to haul kids and groceries around in or a hybrid for commuting."

Genny gave the pad back to him. It was no use. Maybe she'd put an ad in the local paper to see whether she could sell it herself. She sighed and stood. "Thanks anyway. I appreciate you taking the time to give me an estimate."

Billy stood also. "Let me know if I can be of further help. Sure did hate to hear about Agnes Sanders passing. Why, years ago, when I was a kid, she was my Vacation Bible School teacher. Helped me make a cross with seashells on it. I still have that cross. My mother gave it to my wife, who puts it out every Easter. Every time I see it, makes me think of how kind Agnes was."

Billy's eyes misted a bit, so Genny thought it best to say a quick good-bye.

On the drive back home, she decided she didn't even want to bother with the car. It would bring only a fraction of the money she needed. With no way to raise the rest, it seemed pointless. She could sell her car and drive her grandmother's, but her SUV would be worth even less. High mileage. Old. She sighed. She guessed she'd have to go with David's other idea—to search through her grandmother's records.

When she returned home, she went upstairs, opened the closet door where the boxes were stored, and stood back for the torrent of paper sure to stream into the hallway. Mercy. She didn't know whether David was ready for this or not, but he did say to bring the records into his office. Maybe he had help she didn't know about.

One thing was sure, she didn't have time to sift through them on her own.

At least, that's what she thought when she pulled into David's parking lot the next morning with the mishmash of her grandmother's life in the back of the SUV.

Lugging all the boxes from the car into David's office took Genny four trips with David joining her on three and Louvene helping with the last two. They piled them in a corner of David's office, the ill-fitting lids allowing papers to spill over the sides.

Genny blushed to reveal her grandmother's filing system, or rather the lack thereof. "I found these in a closet. But there are also personal notes and letters mixed in. Grandmother tossed all paper in the same box. Like I told you before, though she possessed many amazing talents and attributes, she viewed organization as a waste of time."

David combed his hand through his hair as he surveyed the pile. His smile disappeared as he glanced over at Louvene. "I hadn't quite expected you'd bring in all this." He reached in a box and plucked what appeared to be a recipe from the box. "Chocolate silk pie." He glanced at Genny before he placed it back in the box. "Sounds delicious." Then he shook his head as if trying to clear it. "I checked the date on the security deed, and we're two months short of the time the security deed would've expired, and Lance would have been unable to move on any of this. We can't get a break."

Genny didn't understand much of his legal mumbo jumbo, but she understood enough to know it wasn't good. She regarded the piles before her—it was as if an avalanche covered her. She hoped to avoid wading through all these boxes until later. She'd crammed them back into the closet when she first discovered them because she was already overwhelmed with so many patients at the office. She would dread sifting through who knew how many years of *Worthville Weekly* newspaper clippings, old birthday cards, and recipes. And not to mention dredging up the emotional baggage that went with the memorabilia. "So someone will have to go through these boxes?" Dread seeped into her words.

David raised an eyebrow. "I don't see any way

around it, since we don't know whether your grandmother was aware of the debt." He tried to put a lid back on one of the boxes, but its bulging contents refused to be contained, so the lid slipped off and flopped on the floor. "In fact, *we* will have to go through them."

"We?" Her discouragement mushroomed. "You mean as in you and I? This is going to be a lot of fun." She didn't mean to be so sarcastic.

"Hey, I know it will be tedious, but remember, this is to save your house. She may have paid off the debt, and the payment wasn't recorded. If she kept a receipt, we're all clear. Anyway, it will be worth any short-term aggravation."

Louvene stood near and gave a combination grunt and growl at David's assessment. She guessed Louvene was David's only employee. And not a happy one right now by the look of things. She didn't say anything, but she folded her arms in front of her.

Genny caught David's point. He was trying to help her find the bright spot in a very dark place, but the fact remained she didn't know how she'd do it. "Sorry I'm whining. I'm just trying to figure out how I'll do this with a new job and all. I don't mean to sound ungrateful." On her feet almost the entire day, she'd been exhausted by the time she arrived home because of the unexpected extent of the office workload. Often she didn't get home until eight or nine at night after catching up on the paperwork.

David cast a brief look toward Louvene, whose face bore a scowl. "I understand, but I don't have the staff to do it here. . ." He scanned his tiny office. "Or the space." The boxes spread all the way to the seating area doorway.

Louvene uncrossed her arms and put them on her hips. "No, you don't. You have me going through back files for Mr. Watson's case. I don't know what I'd do if you dumped another project on me."

David shrugged somewhat apologetically. "Small town operation—"

"And I just want to know one thing," Louvene said, interrupting. "Why you didn't figure this out when you saw these boxes in the back of her SUV to begin with. Why did we have to drag all this stuff in here? Looks like anybody with eyes could see it wasn't going to work. Just another example of you not seeing the big picture."

David sighed and did a little blushing himself. "I didn't realize all the boxes were so full and the scope of how many there are..." David stumbled over his words at being rebuked by a senior citizen.

Louvene turned to Genny and with a soft voice said, "Honey, I'm sorry. I'd love to help you, because of Agnes. But I'm not as young as I used to be, and he"— she stopped and nodded toward David—"he has me overloaded already. I'd do it on my free time, but my husband is not well."

"I understand." Genny smiled and touched Louvene's hand. Resigned to what lay before her, she hefted one of the boxes. "I have to do this, no matter how long it takes or how many hours of sleep I lose."

David took the box from her. "Maybe we could do it

at your place. We can start on Thursday, if it's okay with you."

Genny nodded. "Thursday, then. Maybe I can fix a light dinner before we start." She scanned the pile of boxes. "I guess we better cart these back out to my car."

Louvene put her hands on her hips. "I'm going to have to stop by the drugstore on the way home tonight and buy medicated patches for my back. I'm getting too old for stuff like this. I ought to get time and a half for manual labor." She glared at David. "You are something else." She lifted a small box from the stack and trudged out the door as if carrying an anvil. David turned to Genny and shrugged, and even with her heavy heart, Genny found herself stifling a giggle.

THE NEXT MORNING, HARRIET sat on the end of an examination table in street clothes as Genny took her blood pressure. Genny penned numbers on a chart, then started to put her stethoscope in her ears.

Harriet crossed her ankles. "How's it looking?"

Genny put the instrument on the exam table. "In the two weeks since you were last in here, there has been no difference. Are you avoiding salt like I told you?"

Harriet averted her eyes.

Genny studied her a moment. "What aren't you telling me?"

Harriet squirmed on the table. "There's the one thing I eat with salt."

Genny glared at her. "One thing?"

"Cheese crunchies... those little orange crispy snacks..."

"I know what cheese crunchies are. Do you realize they're loaded with salt? And I mean loaded." She put one hand on a hip. "So how many of them do you eat?"

Harriet still avoided eye contact and uncrossed her ankles. "Half a bag a day."

It wasn't often Genny experienced a sense of absolute futility about her work, but this was one of those times. *Why do I try if my patients refuse to cooperate?* There was no way to regulate medication if patients were going to do the absolute opposite of what they needed to do to improve their health. Talk about noncompliant. "That's about a week's worth of your salt allotment in half a bag. No more. Not even a little. Don't even go near the cheese crunchy aisle in the grocery store. Got it?"

Harriet crossed her arms. "You're like grumpy old Dr. Fleming. I guess you medical people are alike, after all. Always trying to spoil somebody's fun. What would your grandmother Agnes say?"

Genny bit the inside of her mouth, trying to hold on to her patience. "She'd say you'd better stop eating the cheese crunchies or else!"

Genny thought for sure another argument would ensue and braced herself for the impending storm, but instead, Harriet erupted into laughter. She pulled a tissue from her purse and wiped her eyes. "Well, I guess she would. Yes, ma'am, I guess she would."

Relieved, Genny retrieved her stethoscope from the table, glad the episode was over. "When I first met you,

you mentioned Grandmother left me a legacy. What did you mean?" If her grandmother stuffed treasure in a mattress or buried it in the backyard, now would be a good time to find out.

Harriet paused a moment before answering, zipping her handbag closed. "You're too young to have met your uncle Bert, aren't you?"

"Grandmother's youngest brother died before I was born." Come to think of it, there hadn't been much discussion about him at home.

"Maybe Agnes mentioned his drinking problem."

Genny put the stethoscope to her ears and listened to Harriet's heart. Out of courtesy, Harriet stopped speaking. As Genny pulled the disk away from Harriet's chest, she tried to recall her grandmother ever mentioning Bert, and she couldn't think of one occurrence. Genny always thought it was because his death was too painful a subject to discuss. Genny shook her head, and Harriet continued her story.

"Anyway, Bert begged his parents for his inheritance early. He got it too and went through it in no time with his high, flashy living—traveling, buying new cars, and squiring the ladies around. Didn't bother to get a job. All the time, he never quit drinking. Then he started working on how to get to your grandmother's money. I don't remember all the details, but through a lot of deception and unscrupulous maneuvers, he did it."

Genny wrote on Harriet's chart but then paused. She didn't know about any of that.

The joy on Harriet's face from earlier was replaced

with lines of grief. "Bert managed to get your great-grandfather to sign a new will before he died, leaving all he owned to Bert. There was a big question as to whether your great-grandfather was of sound mind and body when he did it—memory issues. There was also the question as to whether he was suffering from some sort of duress from Bert. Nevertheless, in the end, Bert wound up with the money."

Genny stared at Harriet in disbelief. Genny always wondered why her grandmother struggled with finances when the stories of her childhood were filled with affluence. Genny assumed there had been some sort of unavoidable financial setback. She never dreamed her grandmother's struggles were a result of cold, calculated greed from her brother. "But how? How could anyone do that to their only sister?"

"I have no idea, but he did. Your grandmother was left with nothing."

Genny shook her head. "I didn't know." Her grandmother kept this heartache close to the vest. Genny sensed her grandmother viewed her role in her life as protector—shielding Genny as much as possible from outside hurt, she guessed because she'd lost her parents at such a young age.

"Agnes struggled to forgive her brother, the hurt was so deep. It took many years for her to let it all go, but by God's help, she finally did about ten years ago." Harriet steadied her gaze on Genny. "She left you a legacy of forgiveness."

Genny was glad Harriet shared this. It broke her heart to think of what her grandmother went through, and she'd been through it mostly alone. Her grandmother seemed perfect to her, and she would have never guessed she held on to a secret like this. But if she was honest, she was disappointed there was no hidden treasure. "Oh" is all she could manage to get out.

Harriet stood. "I have to go. I'm bowling with a few friends."

Genny hadn't seen that information coming. "Bowling?" How did this woman with such unstable blood pressure bowl?

Harriet straightened her shoulders. "Bowled a 204 last week trying to beat Gladiola Spears. She's been the champion in our league two years running. I'm pushing for a 206 today." Harriet grimaced. "I don't know how I'm going to do it, though. Cheese crunchies were my game food."

Genny again stifled a laugh. "If you don't lay off cheese crunchies, the only thing you're going to be pushing is a walker."

Harriet reached for the door handle. "Very funny."

As Harriet headed for the reception area, Genny sighed. As nice as the story was about her grandmother forgiving her uncle Bert, the grim truth was that a legacy of forgiveness couldn't stop a foreclosure.

CHAPTER THIRTEEN

T
HURSDAY EVENING, DAVID SWALLOWED THE LAST of the chicken-salad sandwich Genny made for him and downed a whole glass of sweet tea. Genny hated to eat in the kitchen, but the dining room table was covered. The situation appeared to have no effect on David.

Genny had picked up the chicken salad from Della's Deli on the way home, and it proved to be the right choice on this hot evening. She also stopped at Gray's Grocery and bought a watermelon, which she cut into chunks. It was a small offering in exchange for what would prove a hot, tedious job.

"This watermelon is delicious." David swallowed his last piece of melon. "I need to get one myself. There's nothing like a Georgia watermelon this time of year."

She agreed. The taste of locally grown melons proved to be so much better than those shipped in from other parts of the country.

David wiped his mouth and stood from the kitchen

table. "I guess we'd better get to it. Thanks for the dinner."

"It wasn't much." However, for a man with his affluent background, he gave the appearance of appreciating simple pleasures.

They stood beside her grandmother's dining room table and surveyed the mounds of paper from the boxes she found in the upstairs hall closet. Did David dread the job as much as she did? Why did her grandmother keep some of this stuff? She lifted a page torn from an old catalog with an automatic manicure set circled. She couldn't figure out what might be automatic about a manicure set. Why would her grandmother even consider buying one?

She plucked a yellowed envelope from a box and unfolded the flap to find savings stamps, which her grandmother must have intended to glue in a book. Her grandmother told her she'd obtained a record cabinet in her bedroom with stamps.

Then there was a receipt for a dress from an Atlanta boutique. Genny stared at it. This was the dress she wore her junior year to the prom. The dress was long gone to charity, but here was a tidbit of a reminder. She remembered the day they bought the dress, a sunny Saturday morning in April. They ate lunch at the Swan House as a special treat, and on the way, they sailed along West Paces Ferry past the governor's mansion, with all the windows down and them gawking as if they'd never been to the city before. The dogwood trees were in full bloom, and the air smelled of irises. The special memory caused her breath to catch a bit.

A streak of sentimentality prevented her from letting the receipt go into the recycle bin they were using for discards. She'd have a big contribution for the recycling center when this was over, because Genny decided since they were going through the stuff anyway, they might as well get rid of anything unnecessary. But *necessary* could be a relative term. She slid the receipt under a placemat on the table.

She didn't hesitate to discard many items. "Thirty-year-old light bills." She showed them to David and then chucked them in the recycle bin.

David pointed to a stamp on one of the envelopes. "I wonder if any of these old stamps are valuable. Maybe we ought to put any stamped envelopes aside and have a philatelist look at them."

"A what?"

"A philatelist—a person who collects stamps."

Genny blinked. She considered herself an educated person, but she'd never encountered that bit of trivia.

David's face took on a strained appearance, his jaw tightening. "My dad collected stamps. It was a hobby out of control, though. Almost an obsession. He invested a tremendous amount of money in his stamp collection." David emptied a manila folder and placed the envelope inside. "That's how everything went at our house. It's as if we could never follow a passion for the joy of it. It was always about the return on investment."

It was becoming clearer how David's decision to come to Worthville would have been viewed as irresponsible. Even reckless. After all, Worthville was charming, wonderful, and warm, but it was not where you'd go to make a million. "So you and your dad aren't on such good terms, then?" She hoped she wasn't being too nosy.

David paused as he put another stamped envelope in the folder. "My dad's career goal for me was very specific—corporate lawyer. He was nonnegotiable. When I left to come here, we exchanged words... and I haven't spoken with him since."

The heaviness in David's words weighed on her. "I'm sorry."

David lifted sad eyes to her. "I am too."

Genny tried to think of a way to change the subject. She spied the folder in David's hand. "Would you have the phila—what did you call it again?"

David grinned. "Philatelist."

"Yes, philatelist. Would you have one look at the envelopes?"

David nodded. "We'll take care of it. One of these old envelopes might be the one to stop Saul Lance."

Genny shook her head. A long shot, but at least it was another option.

"Look at this!" David held a yellow piece of paper.

Genny took it from him and scanned the contents of the document, which turned out to be her grandfather's service record. "I can't believe it," she said in wonder.

David ran his finger along lines obviously written by a typewriter. "It shows all the places and dates your grandfather was stationed during the Korean War."

"Illinois, England, Louisiana. I remember grandmother talking about him being an airplane mechanic in the air force."

"Quite a piece of family history. I'm glad we found it." David smiled at her. Their eyes met, and they lingered a moment in that gaze. Then Genny shook her head. *What am I doing?* She'd made a resolution to distance herself from David, and she needed to stick to it. In her present circumstances, that was physically impossible, but she reminded herself she needed to keep her emotional distance.

She slipped the service record under the place mat with the prom dress receipt. Two pieces to keep out of so much—that avalanche feeling again. "What if we don't find anything in these boxes? What are my options?"

David picked up an envelope, and a flicker of something like regret crossed his face. He sighed. "Genny, I'm afraid it's pay off the $20,000 or lose the house."

Genny shook her head. "Some options."

"I know someone who would give you the money."

Genny glared at him. "That subject is off limits."

"Okay, okay." David put his hand on her back. "Are you sure you can't get a bank loan?"

For a moment, Genny drifted back. *How can I ever forget the phone call?* She remembered asking the woman at the bank, "$40,000 in credit card bills? How could he do this to me?" As if the woman on the other end of the line had any idea how Kurt could be so hateful. As if some stranger could explain how he could have spoken words of endearment to her and at the same time have been pulling the rug out from under her.

"Genny, are you still with me?" David asked,

bringing her back to the present. "Trust me. I can't get a loan."

THE NEXT MORNING ON Saturday, Genny and Al stared at the decrepit back steps as a female cardinal called to her mate in a maple tree overhead. "You did such a good job repairing the screen door, but what can be done about these? Do you think we'll have to tear them down and start over?"

Al moved over to inspect the steps, bending and twisting to see over, under, and around boards nailed down decades ago. Many of them were warped and coming off the step support. Others were split and crumbling in places. "These steps ain't been worked on in so long, they're about rotted through." Al stroked his beard. "I believe I will have to start over."

"Grandmother told me your dad built these steps back in the day. Lester was quite the handyman, wasn't he?"

"He was at that." Al's chest expanded in pride.

The brighter male cardinal swooped overhead to the limb where the female rested. Genny shifted her attention to Al. "Your dad was always here to do the jobs Grandmother couldn't or wouldn't do after Grandfather died." She eased down on the shaky back steps. "Sometimes I think she made up projects for him to do to keep him around."

Al grew thoughtful. "They were mighty close. I reckon my dad got lonely after Mom passed."

Genny drifted off a moment. "She missed him when he died." Genny wondered whether in another time and place, her widowed grandmother and the widower Lester might have developed a romance, but in her grandmother's culture, the handyman and the woman of the house didn't do that. Genny guessed they settled for companionship instead.

"We all loved Mrs. Agnes too, and she loved her granddaughter." Al winked at Genny, and Genny smiled at the remembrance. "I was hoping after I retired from the factory, I'd get to work for her too, but she went to meet her Maker before I could. Mighty glad to be helping you, though." Al pulled a measuring tape from his pocket. "I'll get right on these steps, but I can't work late. Have to get to little Lori's ballet lessons."

Genny never saw a grandfather more devoted to his granddaughter. "How old is Lori?"

A big grin formed on Al's face. "Six and about the best blessin' ever happened to our family." He paused a moment and fiddled with the tape measure. "Adopted. Sick when she was little, so we're mighty thankful she's able to dance."

Genny smiled. "I can see you're proud of her. Leave whenever you need to. I have work to do in the house." Genny gingerly covered the steps to the back door, hoping they'd hold for a little longer as Al began measuring for supplies. Her grandmother would be proud of her and Al for the pains they took in getting this house back in order.

Every time she thought about what Saul Lance was trying to do, her resolve increased. No one was going to take it away from her. She'd make sure of it. *But how?*

CHAPTER FOURTEEN

THAT EVENING, GENNY TOOK A BITE of her grilled salmon. Flaky, light, and good if she did say so herself. She glanced across the table at Catherine. "So Don took the kids to the movies?"

Catherine savored a bite of her asparagus. "Yes, they went to the new talking walrus movie. Your invitation couldn't have come at a better time. I was in need of a mom's night out. How'd you have time to do this?"

"I decided to take a break from plowing through Grandmother's financial records this afternoon and have a little fun. I was about to lose perspective. I've been working so many hours at the practice too."

Genny never had kids, so she didn't have any firsthand experience with what Catherine was going through, but she'd seen patients who struggled with the stress of being the sole caregiver for several small children. It was a season of life and would pass, but many of the mothers she'd seen fell into self-neglect during this time and needed a little TLC themselves.

Genny extended a tray toward her. "More salmon?"

Catherine nodded, took the platter, and served herself. "I thought you said you weren't a good cook. This food tastes great."

Catherine's comments might be attributed to the perspective that someone else's cooking often tasted better. "I think you'll find my cooking repertoire somewhat limited. Don't be surprised if the invitations stop coming. It means I don't have anything else to serve you." Genny might work on her cooking skills, though. She liked the sense of community that food could bring to life.

Catherine grew serious. "I'm wondering when someone else might occupy your time. Has David asked you out yet? I see the way he looks at you."

Genny swallowed a bite of roll. Was David looking at her any special way?

She could feel Catherine studying her and anticipated the inevitable question. "Well, has he?"

"We did take a drive in the country, which turned out to be a disaster."

Catherine wiped her mouth with a paper napkin and put it on the table. "A handsome guy like David? How could it be a disaster?"

It was a legitimate question. David was handsome, and what was it about his smile that made her go weak in the knees? "We got stuck and were forced to walk miles to find a phone because we didn't have any bars. I wore a sundress and heels."

Catherine frowned. "Oh." She picked at her food a moment. "But wasn't it great spending all that time with him while you were walking?" Catherine could be absurdly optimistic sometimes.

"No, because I was too busy picking pebbles out of my sandals, wiping my bleeding, briar-scratched legs, and trying to shield my eyes from the sun." Then she added her go-to phrase. "I don't have time for a relationship anyway."

Catherine took another bite of mashed potatoes and grew thoughtful. "But you have time for me."

Busted. Why did Catherine have to be so smart? "That's different. He is coming over to help me sort through Grandmother's financial records, though. Nice of him, since he said he'd help me on a friendship basis. No charge at all."

"Nice? It's unheard of. Do you get how much he bills for an hour of work?"

Catherine waited for a response, but Genny shrugged.

"A lot. That in itself says he's interested in you." Catherine started to say something else but stopped and reconsidered.

"What is it?" Genny asked.

"There's more to David than you know. We have mutual friends, and well… just be careful of judging him based on what you see. There's much more to his story than meets the eye, but he needs to be the one to tell you."

Wow, what was Catherine saying? Was David hiding something? She didn't feel she should push Catherine for more info, so she decided to change the subject. "So Al changed the dryer vent. No more mice."

Catherine nodded. "I'm relieved. I'd hate to have to make a quick exit and leave this food behind." She took a big bite of her roll. "Hey, tomorrow is Sunday. Why don't you come to church with us? You know David comes to the same church."

Genny didn't miss the hint about David. "Oh... well..." What to say? "I have so much to do, you know, with everything closing in like it is."

Catherine studied her a moment. "Another time, then."

"We'll see."

Long after the sun dipped behind the Georgia pines that evening, Catherine sauntered across the road to her house. She glanced back before crossing the road, and Genny waved at her.

To her left, Genny observed Elizabeth roosting on the porch swing as usual. She needed to get Elizabeth a more suitable place to lay her eggs, like a henhouse. She was going to forget to get them one day, and someone, like her, would have a seat and find herself in an eggy mess. Maybe Al could build one after this foreclosure mess was resolved.

Genny hoped the evening provided a respite for Catherine. If laughter were a cure for the weary mother, then Catherine should be in tip-top shape. Maybe she felt better too. They shared crazy college stories and found they had a common dislike for eight o'clock classes in the winter. Especially if they were world history. They went over Agnes's eccentricities, including her affinity for all things chicken, right down to the chicken mailbox cover, which cackled when opened. She didn't want the foreclosure to be the topic for the entire night, so she waited until right before Catherine left to tell her about it. It'd been a long time since Genny connected with a friend like Catherine. And maybe she would go to church with her sometime, but then again, maybe not. She still couldn't figure out why God allowed all the heartache that Kurt caused her. This was such a big thing in her life, yet she never mentioned Kurt to Catherine. She couldn't. It was still so painful—and embarrassing. Maybe more embarrassing than painful. She hated to admit how foolish she'd been.

Catherine didn't ask much about her past. Maybe she sensed ghosts back there and didn't want to pry. Maybe in the same way Connie saw when she was having a bad day. If Catherine did know, she was grateful for her discipline in not saying a word about it. Genny didn't like to talk about Kurt.

She was direct about other matters, though. "A handsome guy like David," Catherine had said.

But Kurt was handsome too. He'd charmed her from the first moment she met him. For so long, it was as if there was no other man in the world but Kurt. He did everything right. He was attentive, considerate, loving, encouraging. Even though he was in a cubicle job with a software manufacturer, he never appeared threatened by her job.

But she'd never forget reading the last letter from him, which contained the line that haunted her until this day. "It's over, Genny." She didn't know that was only the beginning of the dominoes that were about to fall.

Genny shook her head and moved to the kitchen to

finish cleaning after dinner. She turned the radio to a local station to try to drown the thoughts in her head. The song playing had come out about the same time she and Kurt started dating. They often said the songwriter must have written it for them. Genny switched off the radio and sat at the kitchen table. *How was I so deceived?*

THE NEXT SATURDAY, GENNY studied the new steps Al built. He exemplified the same pride of workmanship his dad had. She could tell by the way he'd taken the extra time to reinforce the handrail. In fact, its construction appeared it might hold back a small elephant from tumbling over the side. "You're quite the carpenter."

Al grinned. "Thank you, ma'am. My dad taught me everything."

Genny handed him a check. "I hope this will cover the supplies and your time." She hesitated a moment, dreading to say the next words. "I appreciate all you've done, but I won't be making any more improvements until I see what's going to happen. Just keep the grass mowed." Genny thought of the henhouse she wanted. But no use if the chicken was going to have to go somewhere else.

The expression on Al's face changed to one of puzzlement. "What do you mean, ma'am? What's going to happen?"

Genny grabbed the handrail on the steps. "I mean someone's trying to foreclose on my house."

Al's brow furrowed. "But, ma'am, I know for a fact the house is paid for. Mrs. Agnes told my dad. How could anybody do such?"

"It's kind of a long story—something from very long ago came up, and someone took advantage of it. I'm sure it's no one you know." Genny couldn't imagine Al being friends with someone as underhanded as Saul Lance.

"Sure am sorry." Al picked up his toolbox. "I guess I'll see you next week, then." He started toward his truck and then turned back to Genny. "Almost forgot. Found some things in the shed when I was straightenin'. I thought you might like to take them inside before they get ruined." Al put his toolbox down again and strode to the shed. He reached inside and removed frames. "I believe these here is what you'd put canvas on to paint a picture."

He brought them to Genny, who was still standing at the base of the stairs. Genny blew dust off the top of the frames. "My grandmother worked as an artist over fifty years ago—must have been left over from then. I can't believe they lasted so long out there in the shed."

Al shook his head. "Don't mean to argue, but these frames ain't old. I know wood, and I'd guess they ain't got more than a few years on them."

Genny stared at the frames and tried to understand what Al was saying. "A few years? You found these where?" This whole thing was like trying to put a jigsaw puzzle together but with pieces thrown in from another puzzle. So many elements didn't fit.

Genny followed Al to the shed, and he pointed to a

corner. "Right there."

Genny considered the corner, glanced at Al, and then back to the corner. *What is going on?*

CHAPTER FIFTEEN

S UNDAY AFTERNOON, GENNY TOOK A HANDFUL of winter coats from the guest room closet and piled them on the bed atop the rest of the closet's contents. The bed sagged under the weight, and Genny dreaded sorting through all this before placing the remainder back in the closet. She searched the top of the closet, knocked on the sides and back to make sure there wasn't some mysterious hidden panel, and sat right on the floor to think on the situation.

It wasn't as if Genny left ten years ago and never came back. She'd been in this house numerous times over the years, and she never encountered any evidence her grandmother took up painting again. But what about the paintbrushes and the canvas frames? Could she have been storing them for someone else?

Genny picked up a wool bouclé coat that she remembered her grandmother wearing to church on Sunday. It was a deep cranberry, and her grandmother wore a beautiful silver leaf broach on the collar. Genny held the collar to her face, and the lavender notes of her grandmother's signature fragrance still lingered in the fabric. The old familiar ache intensified. With all her schooling and her experiences working with others, she didn't understand grief. With a mind of its own, it would come or go on a moment's notice. She closed her eyes against it... it was still coming. She slid to the floor with the coat in her hands.

It couldn't be avoided, so she tried to embrace it for the companion it was today. Forever digging through her grandmother's possessions sure kept it going. She'd emptied every closet that could hold even the smallest painting in this house. She explored under all the beds. She even looked under the mattresses. But there was nothing.

Nothing.

She'd even climbed in the dusty attic just in case. She thought Lester emptied the attic years ago, because her grandmother foresaw the time when she wouldn't be able to navigate the creaky fold-down stairs. Together, they either gave away or disposed of the castoffs. So as expected, all Genny found were dust bunnies and stacks of magazines.

This business with the canvas frames didn't make sense. In fact, not much in her life did make sense.

Genny stood and placed the coat back in the closet. Too many memories associated with it. She couldn't let go of it now, maybe not ever.

THE NEXT TUESDAY EVENING, Genny tossed a handful of envelopes in the recycle bin and peered at David in frustration. "I've searched the whole place and can't find any paintings. Why would she have painting supplies if she wasn't painting?" He did that hair-raking thing with his fingers and turned to her. A loop of curly hair fell across his forehead. She was tempted to swoop the strand away from his face. She shook herself, trying to throw off the impulse.

David regarded her in a curious way. "Are you okay?"

"Fine, I'm fine." *Game face. Game face.*

David was speaking again. "Back to your question. Maybe she intended to start again but never followed through."

Genny forced her gaze away from David's hair and to a list of hardware store supplies her grandmother wrote. *Why would she keep it?* Genny tossed it in the trash. "But I found paintbrushes in the laundry room smelling of fresh turpentine."

"She could have painted anything with those brushes." David squinted at the paper in his hand. "Here's a grocery list, which is very old."

Genny laughed. "Yeah, I found a list from the hardware store. How do you know the list is old?"

"From the look of this, money was tight because she's adding up how much each item will cost. The first item on the list is a loaf of bread. It's cheap."

Genny took the grocery list. "I see what you mean." Money was often tight. In retrospect, she didn't understand how her grandmother managed.

She remembered Harriet's story about her uncle Bert stripping her grandmother of her inheritance. Here was proof of her struggle. How did she forgive him of such a thing? By God's help, Harriet had said. Genny could sure use God's help, but how would she get past that business with Kurt? It had made it hard for her to pray and hard to believe that things could ever be right again.

Genny shook her head to shift her thoughts back to the painting business. "About the paintbrushes." She scanned the room around her. The paint job was so old she couldn't even move a picture on the wall because it'd leave the outline of the frame against the faded paint, so Genny didn't think the brushes could have been used in the house. "Do you see anything that looks as if it's been freshly painted?"

David studied his surroundings. "I see your point."

Genny opened a decade-old plant catalog and thumbed through it. The dog-eared pages indicated her grandmother's strong interest in peonies at the time. Across the years, her grandmother's gardening interests had ranged from roses to day lilies to hostas, although there wasn't much shade around to provide the environment the plants demanded. Her grandmother had been a strong student of plant catalogs, and Genny was certain this might be the first of many filed away in these boxes.

She reached the last page and tossed the catalog. Stories she'd read of elderly people hiding their money in newspapers drove the compulsion to scrutinize every single piece in the boxes. She didn't think her grandmother was too eccentric, but with this mysterious painting business, well… she was beginning to wonder whether her knowledge of her grandmother was as thorough as she thought.

She directed a question at David, knowing he didn't have an answer. "So if she painted, where did she do it, and where are the canvases?"

David shrugged as he plucked a school photo of Genny from his stack. "Well, isn't this cute?" He held the photo close to his face, inspecting it.

"Let me see." Genny moved over next to him to see the photo. It appeared to be from sixth grade, as Genny remembered the green jumper she wore. "Look at those freckles. Glad a few of them faded."

David turned to her, and at such close proximity, Genny caught a whiff of his woodsy aftershave, and an unmistakable electrical current went up her spine. They were almost nose to nose. "I like your freckles," he said. For a moment, they seemed frozen. She held her breath.

Then Genny jerked away and pretended to become interested in a recipe for pickle relish she snatched out of the box she was working on. David stood like a statue for a moment or two. When at last he moved, he placed the photo on the table between them and went back to sorting through his box.

"Maybe your grandmother sold the paintings," he said.

"What did you say? Oh yes, the paintings. Maybe she did." She'd forgotten all about them as she tried to catch her breath.

For the rest of the evening, Genny stayed on her side of the table. If she could have, she would have drawn a line between them and put a sign over it that read, "Do not cross." If she needed to examine anything David found, she extended her hand for him to give it to her. What was it she said to Catherine when she first met her about letting her guard down a little? Because right now, she was putting her guard up. And she thought she had good reason to do so.

When David left that evening, she thanked him... in a professional way. Taking his cue from her, he did likewise. "Sorry we didn't discover anything," he said as he left.

As she watched him pull out of the driveway, she had to wonder whether he was correct. It seemed to her they did make a discovery, and she had a flutter in her heart to prove it, but it certainly wasn't what she had been looking for.

CHAPTER SIXTEEN

O N THURSDAY MORNING, CLARICE SCANNED HARRIET'S forehead with a thermometer as Genny put a blood pressure cuff on Harriet's arm.

"Why do you have to take my temperature? Do I look like I have a fever?" Harriet twitched at the attention and pushed Clarice's hand away.

"We're being thorough. Don't want anything to slip through the cracks," Genny said.

Harriet rolled her eyes while Genny pumped the cuff and checked her pressure. Clarice once more tried to get an accurate reading for her temperature. "How about being thorough with somebody else? I have things to do and places to go."

Clarice sighed as she said, "Her temperature is normal, I think." She glared at Harriet.

Harriet shook her head, brushing her off.

Genny took the cuff off Harriet's arm, trying to ignore the drama. "Your pressure is a little better today, but it's still not where I want it to be."

Harriet narrowed her eyes. "I think coming in here every week is what's running it up."

Genny shook her head. "Right. That's it. Doesn't have a thing to do with what's going in your mouth." Genny paused a moment. "Speaking of what's going in your mouth, how are you doing with the cheese crunchies?"

Harriet grunted in disgust. "Put paprika on low-salt rice cakes to at least give them a little color and flavor. Tasted like spicy thick cardboard."

Genny tried to keep herself from laughing. "Glad to hear it." She decided to change the subject. "Do you remember Grandmother Agnes talking about painting?"

"Yes, before Lester died. He couldn't do it—getting too old. She got two of his sons to paint the house. They did a real good job and—"

Genny interrupted. "I don't mean house painting. She worked as an artist when she was younger, and I thought she'd stopped painting, but I've found evidence to suggest otherwise."

Harriet thought for a moment. "I don't remember her mentioning it."

"You don't think she could have sold them, do you?"

Harriet put a hand on a hip. "What? As little as this town is, don't you think I would have known if Agnes sold paintings? I'd been mad as a hornet if I didn't get first choice. Everybody in Worthville loved Agnes and would have wanted a painting too."

"That's right," Clarice said in agreement. "Agnes

had a lot of fans in this town." Clarice put the thermometer back in the side-counter drawer.

Genny jotted a few numbers on a chart. "Maybe David was right, and she was thinking about painting again but never got around to it."

Harriet jumped off the table. "I'm thinking about getting to the bowling alley. Are we through?"

Genny waved her out.

Harriet grabbed her purse, moved toward the door, and then spun back around. "Don't forget about that legacy."

Genny nodded and sighed. Then she called after Harriet, "I better not hear you've been eating those cheese crunchies."

THAT EVENING, CATHERINE TURNED up her lip and plucked an old telephone bill from a box. "How long did you say you and David have been at this?" Catherine's usual chipper demeanor faded somewhat as they plowed through stacks of paper. "This is too much like work."

"Three nights this week." Genny crashed into a chair and could see Catherine studying the mounds yet to be examined.

"It's going to take forever." She turned to Genny with dread in her eyes.

Genny supposed digging through old documents was not apt to appeal to Catherine, who experienced more than her share of domestic chores with two little ones. She'd hated to ask her, but David was unavailable tonight, and she didn't want to let up on the project. Besides, she thought it a good idea that she and David take a little break from each other. She hoped she and Catherine could make something fun out of the job. "I don't have forever—a month or so until Lance forecloses." Genny tried to keep the pressure in check, but the lid threatened to blow on all this.

Catherine turned back to the table. "So we're searching for proof your grandmother paid off the debt to Boyle?" She shuffled a few pieces of paper around.

"Right."

Catherine stared at something in her hand.

Genny's hope rose. "What? Did you find something?"

"Did I?" Catherine held the scrap of paper for Genny to see, her eyes wide.

"A receipt?" Genny grew excited and rose from her chair to get a closer viewpoint.

"No, it's her recipe for peanut-butter cookies. Those were the best treats. Can I make a copy of this? The kids always loved when Agnes brought over peanut-butter cookies, and I never have been able to find a recipe that compared with hers."

Genny stared at Catherine a moment, both unbelieving and crestfallen. "Be my guest." Her grandmother's recipes were so popular, maybe she needed to put a cookbook together. At this point, maybe it was the only way she could extract money from this mess.

They continued plowing through the paper without

speaking for a while; then Catherine spoke again. "Here's something interesting."

Annoyance began to build in Genny. "Let me guess—her lemon pie recipe?" She was beginning to wonder whether having Catherine help had been a big mistake.

"That would be great, but this is a receipt from a year ago." Catherine waved the small scrap of paper.

Genny couldn't figure out how these things became so jumbled. They'd be looking at receipts from twenty years ago for an hour and then something current would pop up. It's as if the boxes turned over and then everything was randomly put back inside. It might have happened when she opened the closet door during one of her searches, but she doubted that one occurrence accounted for such a mess. "What's it for?"

Catherine waved it in the air. "Art supplies."

Genny hopped to her feet. "Let me see." She took the receipt from Catherine, who peered over her shoulder as she studied it.

"Didn't you tell me you thought she might have started painting again? Well, this proves it," Catherine said.

"Maybe. It's from a store called Artists' Attic in Perdue. The address says Main Street." Genny glanced at her watch. "All those stores in downtown Perdue roll up the sidewalks at six o'clock. It's seven now."

"Well, it's something, isn't it?" Catherine appeared proud of her discovery and her eyes brightened.

Genny nodded. "It is something for sure. I think I'll call anyway. Maybe someone's still in the store." She punched the number written on the receipt into her cell phone and held the phone to her ear.

A man picked up on the second ring. "Artists' Attic. Jim Rogers," he said in a low bass.

Genny gave Catherine a thumbs-up, and Catherine clapped her hands in delight.

"Hello, I'm Genevieve Sanders. Agnes Sanders was my grandmother, and I—"

Jim interrupted. "Did you say *was*?"

"Yes, she died a few months ago."

The silence grew on the other end, and then at last he said, "I'm so sorry. We wondered why we hadn't seen her around. She was such a favorite here."

"So you remember her?" Finally someone she could connect to this painting mystery.

"Oh my, yes. No one could ever forget Agnes. Every time she came, she brought a story or an anecdote, and we were all laughing before she left."

That was her grandmother all right. Genny nodded at Catherine and smiled at how beloved her grandmother was to everyone who encountered her. Strange. When she lived with her grandmother, she focused on *their* relationship. She never stopped to consider her influence in the greater context. Catherine stepped closer to Genny and put her ear close to the phone so she could hear the other end. "How often did you see her?"

"Three or four times a year. Sometimes more."

"For how many years?"

Jim paused a moment. "Let me think. Well over ten, I believe. I remember because I met her days after I became store manager—ten years ago this month."

Genny shook her head at the almost unbelievable news. Finally a breakthrough. Her heart stepped up its pace.

Catherine squeezed her arm in excitement.

"You wouldn't happen to know whether she was buying the paint for herself or someone else, would you?"

The voice on the other end said, "For herself, of course."

Genny thanked Jim and hung up the phone. She and Catherine hugged at the wonderful news. Who would have believed it?

Catherine pulled away and bounced on her heels, a big smile plastered on her face. "Ten years," she said. "Why, she could have painted Monet's Water Lilies or the Sistine Chapel in that amount of time."

"Yes, she could have. But where in the world are these paintings?"

Catherine's gaze darted back and forth as if searching for an answer. "I know—a storage facility."

"No bank records for a storage facility," Genny said.

Catherine looked down a moment. "A friend's house?"

"Harriet is one of her closest friends, and she doesn't know a thing about it."

Catherine leaned on the table a moment. "I'm out, but I'm going to keep thinking about this."

Genny hugged her again. "You're a good friend, but let's call it a day. I think we've had enough excitement tonight."

As Genny watched Catherine cross the road to her house, tiny glimmers of light shone through her neighbor's distant windows. When the front door opened, a shaft of light spilled out onto the front lawn from the house, setting the yard aglow. Oh, how she hoped this slip of paper Catherine found was going to be like that door opening, sending a flood of light into her dim situation.

CHAPTER SEVENTEEN

G ENNY GRIPPED THE STEERING WHEEL AS she sat in her SUV in front of David's office. The turn-of-the-century feed store conveyed a charm that was one of the reasons she loved Worthville so much. Whether she wanted to admit it or not, the man inside held a certain charm too, and that was perhaps why she found herself circling back to him whenever a new wrinkle occurred in this whole saga with Saul Lance. She wanted to believe David was her friend, but did he need to hear about every development? Before Genny could answer the question for herself, she unlatched the car door and went inside.

"Well, hello there," Louvene called when she entered. "Bet you want to see David, and you're in luck too. His last client just left, and he doesn't have another appointment for a whole hour." Louvene smiled, stood, and ushered Genny into David's office without even knocking. "You have company," she said, nodding to Genny. Genny held back a giggle at Louvene's usual take-charge attitude.

David put down the contract he was studying, stood, and motioned toward a chair. "Great. Have a seat."

Genny did as instructed, and before she could stop herself, she spilled out the events concerning the receipt. "But where are the paintings? She was talented, and they'd be worth a fortune." She didn't expect an answer. She was venting.

David shook his head. "And Harriet doesn't have any insight?"

Genny ignored his question. "Maybe she sold them at an auction, someplace like Atlanta. Some big place where people here wouldn't find out about the paintings."

David followed with his postulation. "Maybe she used another name. But what would she have done with the money? We've found no evidence in her records to indicate she made deposits other than the usual ones."

They'd tried to reconstruct her grandmother's finances from her income tax returns. Year after year, they were pretty much the same, given her fixed income. Wouldn't her grandmother have reported the income? She was so honest in every other way. But what if she hadn't?

Genny brightened. "Maybe she put the money in her mattress, and I've been sleeping on my salvation the whole time."

THE NEXT SATURDAY MORNING, Genny was going to have to turn the house upside down one more time even though she'd put her head under every bed, into every closet, and inside every cabinet. She was bound to get the grief stirred up again too. She dreaded the whole process.

This time, she was trolling for currency, the kind she could use to pay off the debt, something very green. She tried to use a system. David said the day before that he'd help her. Why, she had no idea. Who would volunteer for this kind of torture? As she sat making a checklist, his car pulled into the driveway. Elizabeth squawked off the porch as he approached. Elizabeth appeared to be working through trust issues herself with David. Every time he came over, she acted as if a fox ventured into the yard.

"Come in," she called before he even knocked.

He flashed his winning smile when he stepped inside. "Ready for a treasure hunt?"

"Ready or not," she said, holding her checklist. "I figured you could take the downstairs, and I'll take the upstairs. I listed places we need to check. But if an idea occurs to you that I don't have on the list, have at it. What I dread most is splitting the mattresses."

David raised his eyebrows. "You're going to open those things?"

"You'd better believe it." Since Genny didn't know about the paintings or Uncle Bert, what other information might she have missed?

They went their separate ways, and she went upstairs to face the mattress in her room. She examined it a moment to see whether there were any unusual-looking seams, maybe where someone had opened the mattress to hide something, but none were apparent. So she grabbed the box cutter and sliced into the striped mattress ticking, making a long cut along the side. Then she dug out some batting and reached inside to see whether anything felt out of the ordinary. She tried not to think about the years of dust mites and other critters that might have accumulated in it. Why hadn't she worn a mask to do this? After a few minutes it became apparent there was no money in this mattress anyway. Rats, but at least she had two more to go. The possibility of discovery and the gross factor collided in her mind.

After being upstairs for a couple of hours, Genny decided to check on David's progress. She didn't mind getting a break from the heat either. With no attic insulation, the temperature was beginning to climb. Plus, all the heat from downstairs came up, and she was starting to feel as if she were in a broiler. She slept with a fan blowing on her at night as well as a window air conditioner operating at full blast to keep from drowning in perspiration on days like this. She didn't remember it being this hot when she was little. All that time up North must have changed her thermostat.

How was she ever going to get the cotton batting back in the mattresses she'd sliced open? She'd have to brush up on her sewing skills to rectify the situation. She was pretty good at putting stitches in people, but regular sewing was something else.

As she went downstairs, wiping her forehead on the back of her arm, rustling sounded from the kitchen.

When she stepped through the door, she was surprised to find frozen food covering the kitchen table and David about standing on his head in the old chest-type freezer her grandmother bought when Genny was a little girl. What was he doing?

"David?"

He stood and turned to her. "You said to check if there was any place not on the list. I thought this freezer might hold a clue." He held an unidentifiable frozen package. "She has ground beef in here with a ten-year-old date on it."

Genny tried to hold back her laughter at the sight of David, the Worthville attorney, almost frostbitten, clutching old hamburger meat. The big freezer was the last frontier in this house. She hadn't even cracked the lid since she moved back. She'd kept her frozen food in the freezer section of the refrigerator. "I'm not surprised. Grandmother didn't hold to expiration dates. She always said we throw away too much food in this country and, if it didn't smell bad, you ought to eat it."

David scrutinized the ground beef. "Well, are you going to?"

"Not a chance," she said.

"I'm going to need a garbage bag." David surveyed the mess on the table. "Make it two."

Genny retrieved the brown bags, and together they sifted through stacks of meat and vegetables. They found two bags marked "ham bones." Genny guessed her grandmother intended to make soup from them but never got around to it. Genny tossed them.

She cooled from her second-floor heat wave and

retrieved a pair of woolen gloves so she could stand the frigid temperatures handling all the cold packages. What she needed, though, was cold, hard cash.

David reached back into the bottom of the freezer. "What is this?" He pulled out a plastic bag with two brushes in it.

Genny stepped over and took them. From an artist friend in New York, she learned when using oils, if you didn't have time to clean brushes, you could put them in the freezer, thaw them, and reuse. That way, they wouldn't be ruined if you didn't have time to clean them, and it saved on paint by being able to pick up where you left off. Did her grandmother put these in the freezer and then forget about them under mounds of frozen foods? Judging from where David found them, near the bottom and under the decade-old ground beef, they had been there for years. More evidence she was painting, yet no paintings.

David echoed her thoughts. "Those must have been in there for a long time."

Genny nodded, tossed the brushes in a garbage bag, and sank into a kitchen chair. "But where are the canvases?"

David threw up his hands, conveying his frustration.

With no answers in sight, they continued with the freezer cleanout. After stuffing the two bags, David hefted one in each hand. "I'll stop by the dump and unload these. You don't want these in your garbage can when old meat starts defrosting. You'll have dogs from miles around coming to pilfer your trash." He headed out to his car, and when he returned, he closed the empty freezer lid. They'd found everything expired but two bags of frozen strawberries. "I assume you didn't find much upstairs either."

Genny shook her head. "Not a thing." She dreaded dealing with the cotton batting.

He handed her the list she'd given him, moved to the sink, washed his hands, dried them on a towel, and turned to her. "I guess I'd better be going. Sorry."

"Yeah. I have to get back upstairs and figure out how I'm going to mend a couple of mattresses."

David laughed. "I'd offer to help, but sewing has never been in my skill set."

Genny nodded and smiled. "Thanks anyway."

David put his arm around her shoulder to console her and pulled her close. She found herself slipping an arm around his waist. She didn't want to admit how much she enjoyed being close to him.

Later that evening, as Genny sat on her bed, stitching the last twelve inches of a slice in her old mattress, Catherine looked on, holding the material together for her to sew. Genny had called and asked whether, after she got the kids to bed, she could come over for a few minutes and help. Catherine proved to be a real friend through all this. Genny was going to owe her big time. Maybe she could babysit so Catherine and Don would have alone time. At the least, she needed to tell Catherine about Kurt, so as she sewed, she unloaded the whole terrible story about him writing her a letter to tell her it was over.

"He dumped you in a letter? What a creep,"

Catherine said her eyebrows furrowed.

Genny gave the thread a tug, pulled a stitch through, and tied off a knot. "That's only the beginning. After that, I found out he'd run up all my credit cards, drained my accounts, and destroyed my credit. You can see why I'm reluctant to jump into another relationship."

"Oh, no wonder. I can't imagine someone being so underhanded and mean. Why, if I had been there, I would have had to let him have it." Catherine paused for a moment. "That kind of meanness sounds like someone else I know. Do you think Saul Lance and Kurt are related?"

Genny let go a cynical laugh. "They do have a lot in common, don't they?" As Genny rethreaded her needle, she wondered where Kurt was. Probably scamming another unsuspecting nurse practitioner. She had to wonder whether he had a pattern of searching out professional woman with good incomes so he could bankrupt them.

Genny stitched a few more inches and finished the job.

Catherine held a wad of leftover batting. "So what are you going to do with this extra stuffing? Don't you think it will make the mattress flatter not having it all back in?"

Genny thought a minute. "It might, but I couldn't get it all to go back in and still sew it together. Maybe these old mattresses were overstuffed."

"Maybe," Catherine agreed in an unconvinced way. "I don't think people put money in mattresses anymore."

Genny narrowed her eyes at Catherine. "No kidding. And by the way, unless you want about a hundred new neighbors, I need you to help me think of where else I might find paintings or money."

Catherine grew pensive. "Barn?"

"Al checked it."

"Attic?"

"I did it myself. Nothing but spiderwebs and old *TV Guides*. I can't figure out why she saved those things. It's not like the television stations were going to reuse their old schedules. Maybe she liked the pictures—or the articles. Hey, help me get this mattress in position." They maneuvered the mattress around and situated it squarely on the foundation. "There. Done."

As she and Catherine made the bed, Catherine stopped. "What about the space under the house?"

"I crawled under there, but trust me, there's no way Grandmother would have stored anything in that cave of a place. There's barely room for a mouse to run." Genny hadn't even played under the house when she was young because it was scary. Not much had changed since then because she feared she'd run headlong into a rat or opossum. Her grandmother wasn't a fan of dark, dank places either.

Catherine tossed pillows on the bed. "I like neighbors, but Lance's plan is over the top. Sure wish we could think of something to stop all this."

"My brain hurts from trying to generate ideas, not to mention my back from crawling around under the house."

Her cell phone rang on the bedside table, and Genny reached for it. She didn't recognize the number but answered anyway in case it might be a patient.

"Hello, is this Genevieve Sanders?"

"It is."

"My name is Winslow Echols."

"Yes, Mr. Echols. How can I help you?" Genny swiped at mattress stuffing on her clothes.

"I happened to be in Artists' Attic when you called to speak with my friend Jim Rogers. I overheard the conversation. I'm an art dealer in Perdue and thought you might be interested to know that Agnes Sanders contacted me two years ago about selling her paintings."

Genny listened, then froze and looked wide eyed at Catherine. "She contacted you about selling her paintings?"

"Yes. I deal in nonobjective work, so I couldn't help her, but I put her in touch with an Atlanta auction house—Wiersbe's."

"Oh, thank you. This is a tremendous help."

"You're quite welcome. In my brief conversation with her, her gracious personality was evident. I hope this helps."

"It does. It does. Thank you, Mr. Echols." Genny clicked the phone off, feeling she might jump for joy. She turned to Catherine. "You won't believe this," she said and shared the conversation with her.

Catherine put her hand over her mouth in surprise and then hugged Genny. "This is fabulous."

Genny clapped her hands, relishing the news. She could have danced all the way to the depot. "Isn't this great? There are paintings. I can't wait to call."

Catherine clapped her hands too, swept up in Genny's exciting news, but then the joy drained from her face, and she froze. "Or there *were* paintings."

Genny sobered. "What do you mean?"

"Her paintings might have been sold. What if Wiersbe's has already auctioned her work?"

A bad thought. But wait. Genny gestured around her. "And done what with the money?" She echoed the question she'd asked David. "As you can see, nothing has been updated."

Again, as far as she and David could tell, there was nothing in her grandmother's financial records to indicate she realized any extra money. She was 100 percent sure there was nothing hidden in the house. Make that 110 percent sure. If compelled to stick her head under one more bed, take the belongings out of one more closet, or—as she studied the bed they'd made that boasted a decisive sunken spot in it—pilfer through mattress stuffing again, she would scream.

The single bright spot in the whole situation was her complete knowledge of everything in the house. No wondering whether she needed to buy black thread to sew on a button—four spools. Did she need wrapping paper for a friend's birthday present? No—eight varieties in the upstairs closet. Would she be shopping for new Christmas decorations? Not unless she intended to throw out eight boxes her grandmother accumulated. And oh, how could she forget? If anyone in her circle ever needed shower gel, her grandmother stockpiled enough to last into the next decade.

Catherine sat on the side of the bed. "I'm trying to be realistic. Maybe she gave the money away or established a scholarship fund or something."

A scholarship fund? Genny considered Catherine's point. But no. Her grandparents didn't have strong links to a place of higher education. "I think I would have known. That would be big family news." She couldn't believe her grandmother wouldn't have let her in on a philanthropic act like setting up a scholarship. Plus, Genny would have found it when she searched her grandmother's name online. She'd needed to make sure no one was selling paintings by Agnes Sanders somewhere on the World Wide Web.

Genny wanted to believe she understood her grandmother and there was nothing clandestine going on. Still, the way things were going, nothing would have surprised her.

CHAPTER EIGHTEEN

C LARICE ENTERED GENNY'S OFFICE WITH A newspaper in her hand. Her eyes darted back and forth between the newspaper and Genny. Strange behavior.

Genny put Terence Turnstyle's chart on her desk. His blood sugar readings were high, and Genny thought she might send him to a dietician. She suspected he was pulling a Harriet and sneaking around eating food he was supposed to avoid. Her patience ran thin with noncompliant patients. She wondered why they even came in if they weren't going to do what needed to be done.

Clarice stood by her desk, and with one hand, she fidgeted with a swirly blue Murano glass paperweight Genny picked up at the Metropolitan Museum of Art. Genny feared Clarice was about to turn it into a bowling ball. Her behavior made it clear there was something she didn't want to say. "What is it, Clarice?"

Clarice put the paperweight down and came around

her desk. She held something behind her in the other hand, moved toward Genny, knelt, and violated her personal space by a good six inches. "I need to tell you something," she whispered.

What is going on? Clarice had never behaved this way before. There wasn't anyone else in the office, so why was she whispering? It was as if she was about to let her in on an awful piece of gossip. Genny imagined a day never went by that there wasn't some sort of personal tidbits rolling through Dr. Fleming's office, but she never knew Clarice to get involved in such things.

Clarice handed her the newspaper folded back to the legal advertisements. She pointed to one. Genny read the tiny little print and gasped. She couldn't believe it. The legal notice gave the details of the foreclosure on her house. Her home. The one she was about to lose according to this notice. Here for everyone in Worthville to see. Genny turned to Clarice, whose face was lined with compassion.

Genny could feel the blood rising to her face. Shame covered her like a blanket. "People are talking about this, aren't they?"

"I'm so sorry" is all Clarice said, dropping her head.

THAT EVENING, GENNY AND David stood in line at Connie's Coffee and Cones. Genny glanced out of the corner of her eye to see whether anyone shared pitying looks over her situation. But the crowd was mostly middle school girls smitten with an online video. One of them held a phone while the rest of them crowded around watching, licking their dripping cones.

Connie had added a chalkboard to her decor on the back wall, and on it she had written, "'To keep on trying in spite of disappointment and failure is the only way to keep young and brave. Failures become victories if they make us wise-hearted.' —Helen Keller."

Genny considered Helen Keller a wise woman, but how could this disappointment become a victory? Connie came out of the back, spotted Genny, and stepped to the counter. "I've got this," she said to a young woman at the cash register.

Genny paused a moment, then turned to David. "Why don't you go ahead. I'm still thinking." David ordered one scoop of butter pecan and one scoop of black cherry, and when Genny stepped up to order, Connie gave her the most loving gaze. "What will you have, dear? If you like chocolate, I have a new flavor, Choco Chunko, that will bring a smile to your heart."

Choco Chunko did sound good, and Genny could sure use a smile in her heart. "I'll take it—three scoops." She was glad none of her patients were there to see her lack of willpower. "I like your new chalkboard."

"Thank you. I'm always finding quotes I like, as you can see." She pointed to the quotes already hanging in the store. "But I wanted to be able to share new ones whenever I want, so"—Connie waved her hand to the board—"voilà."

"Good idea," Genny said, wondering how Connie was always on point with what was going on with her. When she passed her the cone, Genny almost cried. One reason was that it was so big, she didn't know how she would ever eat the top scoops before the bottom one melted. Another reason was Connie could send a hug through her gaze. She believed if she could stay in the ice cream store for about twenty-four hours, she could get over her worries—much the same way kids were charmed by Connie.

Instead, Genny and David moved down the street a way, sat on a bench outside the depot, and licked their ice cream cones. They both worked on the cones for a while before speaking. Hers required diligence to keep the chocolate from dripping on her white pants. She crunched on one of the pecans in the Choco Chunko and swallowed. "There's something about eating ice cream that's so consoling after a humiliation, don't you think? Connie could make you feel better after about anything."

"Connie does have a special something. Too bad it can't be bottled." David bit off a section of his cone, chewed, swallowed, and sighed. "So here's what happened. The law requires those notices run several consecutive weeks prior to a foreclosure."

She stopped eating her cone. "And you didn't tell me?"

David shook his head. "To be honest with you, I forgot about it with us trying to figure out a way to put an end to this whole business."

"Who reads those notices anyway?" She couldn't imagine reading a newspaper and thinking, *Hey, I think I'll see who's losing their house this week.*

David swallowed the last of his sugar cone. "People

who want to capitalize on others' misfortunes." He paused a moment. "But the average person doesn't read them. The problem is Worthville is such a small town, if someone sees it, they pass along the information, which is what I think happened in your office. My guess is Clarice put a stop to it as soon as she found out."

David was right. Clarice would have put a stop to it. But what if the news had already moved beyond the office? A few cars passed as they sat in silence. Genny shook her head. For a few moments, she tried to not allow herself to be twisted in a knot by all that was happening. "At least the call from Mr. Echols was a good lead."

"It's good he happened to be there at the exact time you called."

Another car passed.

"I have a call into Wiersbe's auction house in Atlanta. I hope I hear something soon."

Talking about the foreclosure went around in a circle. Genny liked things in place. But for so long, her life had reeled out of order. One hard thing after another.

A man walking a German shepherd nearly as big as her grandmother's car crossed in front of them. Genny had thought about getting a dog, but she was concerned it might eat Elizabeth. The chicken was still a living connection to her grandmother, something she loved. Elizabeth must be protected. She guessed she was trying to hold on to anything she possibly could that tied her to this woman who meant so much to her.

She decided to change the subject and turned to

David. "So has Worthville been what you thought it would be?"

"It's not North Atlanta, but I don't want it to be. I was ready for something smaller, something with a sense of place and roots. I guess it's taking me a little longer than I anticipated to get my practice off the ground." He smiled. "You're not alone in your hesitancy to trust me. People around here want to know if I'm one of them. There have been a couple of times I wondered if my dad was right in what he said about me coming here."

"What was that?" Genny finally polished off her cone and brushed her hands together to rid them of crumbs.

David paused a moment as if wondering whether he should tell her. "'You're going to a one-horse town to open a mom-and-pop operation when you could be a real lawyer here in Atlanta.' It always felt like he was saying I became an imitation attorney by moving to Worthville."

This must have been the backstory about David that Catherine was talking about at dinner a while back. "You know that's not true." A real lawyer—Genny could understand how much words like that could hurt coming from someone you cared about. Every time she thought about Kurt's parting letter to her, she winced. In it, he made it sound as if she wasn't enough, that she had failed the relationship somehow. In truth, her bank accounts weren't enough since he'd gone through all the money.

David's face flushed a bit as he appeared to grow

embarrassed over making himself so transparent. However much she tried to hold back, his willingness to be vulnerable drew her to him.

"So do you have any regrets about coming back to Worthville?" she asked. At the same time, they both spotted Saul Lance walking toward them. The usual disgusting toothpick hung out of his mouth. When he passed, he let out a laugh, which grew louder and louder as he moved toward his dirty pickup truck. He got in and roared away. In the still heat of the early evening, he left behind a dusty cloud that settled on them.

They stared after him a moment, dumbstruck. David cleared his throat to speak. "Maybe just one."

CHAPTER NINETEEN

G ENNY LEARNED TUCKER'S TOMES STAYED OPEN until eight a couple of nights a week. David was otherwise occupied tonight, and she wanted to browse the bookstore for a few minutes before going home and facing the dreaded task of searching through more of her grandmother's financial records. She slipped in the door and became aware no customer went unnoticed by Tucker. "Make yourself at home," he boomed from somewhere in the back of the store.

She headed straight for the biography section again and pulled off a volume about famous women in medicine. As she moved to take a seat, Tucker approached her. "I see you have an affinity for the medical field."

"I do," she responded, still in awe of his amazing voice. He tilted his head. "Are you related to Agnes Sanders?"

"I'm her granddaughter."

"I thought so when you came in a few weeks ago.

You have her eyes, and when I saw you with these medical books, I remember she told me she had a granddaughter who was a nurse practitioner." He extended his hand. "I'm Tucker, and Agnes was one of my favorite people."

Genny smiled and shook Tucker's hand. "My grandmother affected many that way. I'm Genny."

Tucker nodded. "It's a pleasure."

He turned to check out a customer, but Genny continued to revel in his resonant voice.

She settled into what was becoming her favorite seat and lost herself in stories. When she emerged from them, she checked her phone—she'd been there an hour. Far longer than she'd planned. As usual. But a heavenly respite. She returned the book to the shelf and waved at Tucker.

"Wait a minute," he said. "I think I have something for you."

"For me?" Genny asked.

Tucker went to the end of the counter, squatted down, and began pulling out books, small boxes, cartons of pens, and other items from under the counter. He reached in the very back and came up with a sack. He dusted it off. "I was right. It says *Genny Sanders* right here on it."

"But what is it?"

"Several months ago, your grandmother came in and bought this book. She said one day you'd be in and I should give it to you. I asked her if she wanted me to ship it, but she said no, just wait till you came in. I almost forgot about it."

Genny opened the sack, and her breath caught when she read the title, *Art in Georgia.*

She opened the book and scanned its contents—all stories about native Georgia artists. She hoped for a note, a message, but she found none. What had her grandmother meant leaving this for her?

Vexed about the book, after she left Tucker's, she decided since she was already so late getting home, she'd take a few minutes to stop by Bodine's Bowling before wading through an ocean of paper. She was procrastinating, but hey, it was fun.

The ball rolled down the alley and smashed into the blue pins, leaving one standing. Genny clapped and shouted, "You get 'em, Harriet."

Harriet wheeled around, spotted Genny standing next to the concession stand, and moved toward her. "Well, look who blew in. My doctor never made a bowling alley call before."

Genny gave Harriet a hug. "I had to see this for myself."

Harriet nodded toward a tall woman wearing a purple bowling shirt with her gray hair in a French twist. "Gladiola over there thinks she has the championship sewn up, but she hasn't seen anything yet." Harriet blew on her hands as if they were blazing hot and then moved back to the lane. She hoisted a ball, sent it flying, and knocked over the other pin. She pivoted and grinned at Genny.

It was hard to miss Gladiola Spears's steely glare directed to Harriet.

Bowling could be serious business.

Harriet strolled over to Genny. "So when are you going to take up the sport yourself?"

Genny looked around. "Me? No, no. I'm not a bowler. A bowling ball would be a dangerous weapon in my hands. I'd be knocking pins down three lanes over."

Harriet laughed. "I bet you'd be a good bowler. We're going to need some more folks on our team in the fall."

Genny questioned bowling in a geriatric league. She would like to be with younger people. "So you're losing some of the team in the fall?" She wondered whether they might be getting too feeble for the sport.

Harriet moved toward the ball return. "Yeah. They're going back to college."

Genny shook her head to process the information. "You have college kids on your team?"

"Well, sure. It takes somebody pretty young to keep up with me."

Genny was glad she wasn't in a clinical setting and could laugh out loud at Harriet's comment.

Genny munched on popcorn, drank two sodas, and chatted with other people who had come to watch the team. She learned the colorful Harriet had many fans. After a couple of hours, Genny picked up her purse and made her way to the bowling alley exit, amazed at what she'd seen and heard that night. Harriet was some bowler. In fact, she felt energized by her example. So she stayed up until one going through her grandmother's boxes. She could sleep late the next morning because it was the Fourth of July. Since the office was closed, she didn't have any plans except to continue with the job that appeared to stretch into infinity. David had taken a last-minute out-of-town trip and wouldn't be back until the next day. She couldn't wait to talk to him about the book her grandmother had left her. Was it a clue? She flipped through the pages again and found the profiles of various Georgia artists and pictures of their work interesting, but she would have found a note from her grandmother about what was going on even more interesting.

Instead of getting to sleep in, she woke up to her cell phone buzzing on the nightstand as first light seeped through the blinds. She hoped it wasn't an emergency. She groaned as she answered the phone. The screen identified the caller as Catherine. What could she want this early in the morning? She grunted a hello.

"Are you awake? We've been up thirty minutes, getting ready for the big day."

Genny shook herself. "Big day?"

"Yes, downtown at the depot. They have all those food trucks that come in from Atlanta and a parade and fireworks. Go with us?"

Genny moaned. Food trucks. Parades. Fireworks. She'd seen the flyers around the office but never gave a thought to going. This sounded like an all-day affair. All she wanted to do was go back to sleep.

"Don't tell me you're spending the day going through old paper again. You have plenty of time. Your grandmother would have had a fit if you stayed inside and missed the Worthville Fourth of July celebration. I bet she didn't miss one her whole life."

Catherine made a good point. It was one of the high

points of the year for her grandmother. But she'd been lax the night before by going to the bookstore and then to the bowling alley. How could she justify taking a whole day off when David was sacrificing his time to help her?

"Please go with us, Miss Genny," Lauren and John asked on the other end of the phone. "Daddy's got to work today."

Catherine was pulling out the big guns to get her to go. How could she say no? "Oh, okay. Give me time to pull myself together?"

"Yay," the kids cried.

"See you in a bit," Catherine said.

It wasn't as if Genny hadn't been to one of these celebrations before. She never missed an Independence Day observance until she went to college.

In thirty minutes, Genny was dressed and in the car with Catherine on the way into town. She managed to tell Catherine about the book between them both answering questions from excited kids in the back seat.

"So why do you think your grandmother left you the book?" Catherine asked.

"I don't know. It's all so weird," Genny said.

"I'd say so. It's like she was trying to tell you something, but what?"

"Mommy, did you remember our bicycles?" Lauren asked.

"They're in the back."

Genny never answered Catherine's question, because the moment passed, but she didn't know what she would have said anyway. When they arrived at the depot midmorning, students were already setting up for the Worthville Wolverines high school band to play their traditional medley of patriotic tunes as they marched along Main Street later. The evening concert would be a real crowd-pleaser too from what she remembered. Red, white, and blue bunting placed around the depot gave it a festive appearance, and most everyone in the crowd was dressed in the traditional colors.

Behind the depot, on the Worthville softball fields, the food trucks arrived in droves. "We've got to scope out everything so we can make our decisions," Catherine said, eyeing the many possibilities. "The lines get kind of long close to noon, so let's eat lunch early."

Elsewhere on the fields, tables loaded with streamers, ribbons, pom-poms, and glittery signs were ready for bike decoration. Even car-riding kids brought their bikes to the depot. As promised, Lauren's and John's training-wheel-bedecked bikes were in the back of the car, ready to be decorated. Catherine told her the kids would queue up behind the Worthville Wolverines marching band. "We'll go back and get the bikes after we make our food selection," Catherine said.

Genny waved to several patients she recognized as she and Catherine made their way toward the food trucks. It was nice to feel part of their lives, something she didn't experience often in New York.

To her surprise, the first food truck they came to sported the sign "Connie's Coffee and Cones." Connie leaned out the window. "Hey, y'all. Come on over."

"So you have a food truck?" Genny couldn't believe it.

"You bet. How would I do all those birthday parties if I didn't? Why, sometimes on Saturdays, I'll have three parties in Worthville, Perdue, and all around." Connie shook her curly locks. "I love the kids, so it's more like fun than work. Even though my store is close to the depot, I thought I'd join the food truck fun."

Genny didn't realize Connie also owned a party business. She was some busy gal. A hard worker.

"It's too early for ice cream, but I have coffee too," Connie suggested. "And muffins with fresh blueberries." She pointed to a tray on the ledge behind her.

Genny exhaled in relief. There had been no time to make coffee before she left. She bought coffee with a blueberry muffin and welcomed the solace of the dark brew as Connie placed it in her hands. When she bit into the muffin, she decided the trip was worth it if for the delectable muffin alone. Connie was a marvel.

Connie handed Lauren and John a coupon for one free scoop to be used at another time. Until then, their excitement about the day almost burst its bounds, but in Connie's presence, they melted into their cherubic personas. "Precious," Connie said.

They were about to move on to check out other trucks when something caught Genny's eye.

Not a truck, but a display. It was Saul Lance cleaned up, standing beside a huge board advertising his Worthville Retreat development. Who let him into this celebration? She didn't think he'd seen her, but from her vantage point, she could tell the picture on the display included her land with his clubhouse sitting right where her house stood. It was as if he already owned it. "I can't believe it," she cried aloud, clinching her fists, her anger twisting a knot in her stomach. She found herself moving toward the man.

Catherine grabbed her arm. "Not worth it."

She stopped and reconsidered. No, it wasn't worth it to get into a shouting match with him around the children. And in front of her patients. It could wreck her credibility. She was a little embarrassed she didn't think ahead. She was thankful Catherine intervened. But still, that man set off combustion in her in a way even the fireworks that night wouldn't match.

CHAPTER TWENTY

THE NEXT EVENING, WHILE GENNY AND David sifted through a decade of her grandmother's personal archives, she chucked another stack of useless paper into a recycle bin and collapsed in a chair. The paper slid off the overflowing mounds onto the floor. It appeared they would have to find another bin someplace. David was a real trooper through this process. Guilt crept over her because she'd taken the day off. "Sorry I didn't get much done yesterday. Catherine and the kids wanted me to go and—"

David held up a hand, stopping her. "Genny, you work ten or twelve hours a day and then come home to this. You hardly put your feet on Georgia soil before you were thrown into fight mode. Please don't apologize. You needed a break."

His understanding caused the tension in her shoulders to melt, and she breathed easier. She hadn't even realized how tense she was, and David's understanding soothed her. The day before was a wonderful day, except for the Saul Lance thing. It took her a while to get over seeing him, but the barbecue she and Catherine decided on helped her recover from her encounter, in addition to the remainder of Connie's blueberry muffin she saved for dessert.

Worthville Retreat? She wanted Saul Lance to retreat to wherever he came from and leave her alone.

She sighed, looking at the stacks remaining. "How far along are we, do you think?"

David stopped thumbing through a wire-bound notebook with so much age on it, Genny thought it might have been around before she was born. He surveyed the situation. "We're about halfway." He sighed at the sight of the full bin. "I'll bring the recycle container from my house, since yours is full."

"Sorry about that. When you live out in the country, there's no recycling pickup, so I have to haul everything to the county center. It's out of the way and one more thing on my to-do list."

"No worries," he said as he picked up a catalog. "This is so tedious, having to examine each seed catalog and pore over every notebook filled with grocery lists to make sure there's not something stuck between the pages that might solve the problem."

"Like a few $1000 bills." She didn't think the large bills were even in circulation anymore, but she sure would like to see Grover Cleveland's face right about now. Once more, the grimness of the situation pressed in on Genny. "We don't have much time left."

David threw the notebook on the table. "We're tired and hungry. Why don't I take us out to eat at Chen's

Chinese, and then we can come back and work a few more hours?"

Genny examined her T-shirt and jeans. "Look at me."

David patted his jeans. "Chen doesn't care. Let's go."

Genny hesitated a moment and then nodded. "Fine. I have something I want to show you anyway."

SHE COULD SAY MANY things about New York evenings.

The lights of Broadway sent a chill along her spine, and the skyline dazzled in the waning light of day. One of her favorite pastimes was walking by lamplit brownstones around Central Park and imagining who lived there, what they might do for a living, what books they read, and the decor in their apartments. She even loved the smell of the city, even though it sometimes amounted to the scent of burnt pretzels from street-corner stands and car exhaust from a steady stream of yellow cabs transporting New Yorkers from one end of the city to another.

But Worthville, Georgia, at nightfall possessed a charm all its own.

Genny and David strolled along Main Street, where twinkling lights outlined the architecture of the depot, the centerpiece of the town. Gas lamps installed on the streets in recent years replicated ones torn down under the guise of urban renewal decades before. Tucker's Tomes featured a giant illuminated globe in the window, while next door, at Connie's Coffee and Cones, assorted brightly lit bulbs in the shape of ice cream toppings worthy of an entertainment park trimmed her window. The colorful paper lanterns at Chen's Chinese created a glowing ambience for patio diners. The whole effect was enchanting. She glanced over at David. Her heart fluttered, and she resisted an urge to grab his hand as they walked. Instead, she adjusted the straps of the tote bag she'd grabbed on the way out the door.

"Why don't we eat outside?" she asked.

"Sounds good to me." He scanned the sky. "Great weather. And it's late enough the temperature has cooled a bit."

There was even a breeze blowing, making the lanterns sway.

After they received their orders, Genny twirled her vegetable lo mein on a fork as a candle glimmered on the table. "This is nice." She pulled out the book about Georgia artists from her tote bag. "While you were gone, I was at Tucker's, and he remembered Grandmother left me something. He dug around under a counter and came up with this." She handed him the book.

He read the title aloud. "*Art in Georgia.* Wow, it's almost like she's sending you a message." He opened the book and flipped through the pages.

"Don't even look. I already have. I thought she might have left a note or something for me. But nothing."

"Right. Maybe one that told us about any paintings she might have done." He handed the book back to her. "Really strange."

She nodded in agreement and put the book back in her tote bag.

He studied her a moment with a pensive gaze. "Glad you came." He paused, his eyebrows furrowed, hesitating as if rethinking his words. "There's something I need to say." He paused again. "Sometimes it feels like you still don't trust me."

Genny stared a moment at her plate. "I guess it's my history getting in the way."

David's brow furrowed. "History?"

Genny took a sip of hot tea and swallowed, debating whether to tell David the whole nasty story. Maybe she'd take the chance. "I was engaged... back in New York. We'd planned to be married this summer."

A waitress came to check on them, but David waved her away, then turned back to Genny. "Go on."

Genny took a deep breath. "So my fiancé, Kurt, thought in preparation for marriage, it would be good if we started managing our finances together, so I added him to my accounts."

David put down his fork, leaving his pepper steak languishing on his plate. "I have a feeling this story doesn't end well."

Genny laughed, which sounded far more cynical than she wanted it to. "I didn't see the red flags. He ran up all my credit cards and drained my bank accounts." She sat back in her chair. "Then he left. Now I'm burdened with repaying the huge balances on the cards, and because I've missed a couple of payments along the way, the companies have raised the interest rates. The burden of debt is almost crushing. Plus, there's no way any bank will loan me money because of it." She looked out the window. "That's why I drive the old SUV and will for some time. When Grandmother left the house to me, it gave me a chance to use what I would normally pay for living expenses and try and pay down the debt. Now Lance is trying to take that away from me."

David reached over and touched her hand. "I'm sorry."

His hand felt warm on hers. Comforting and thrilling at the same time. "If I appear leery, I am. I can't stop thinking about what Kurt did to me. When Grandmother left me the house, as sad as I was over losing her, she gave me this wonderful gift and it was like an answer to all my problems. I decided to move back here. But as you know, even more problems have arisen."

David nodded. "You moved to Georgia, but you've brought a lot of New York back with you. Like you're still carrying all of that around as well as this Saul Lance stuff."

Genny pulled her hand away from David's and concentrated on her food.

"I shouldn't have said that." David stared at his plate.

"It's hard to let it go. Because I didn't see it coming, I don't trust others, and I don't trust myself sometimes." Genny took a deep breath. "After all, I was the one who allowed him to do what he did." Here she was in the health-care field, the person in charge of helping others solve their problems, yet she wavered in personal decisions. She needed to change the subject. "On a lighter note, have you ever seen Harriet Glaussen bowl?"

The waitress returned to sweep their plates away and leave them fortune cookies.

David exhaled as if relieved to move on to other subjects too. "She's a force of nature."

Genny unwrapped a fortune cookie, broke off a piece, and chewed. She let the paper fortune drop to the table without looking at it. "There's quite a rivalry between Harriet and Gladiola Spears."

"You didn't look at your fortune." David pointed to the piece of paper on the table.

Genny hadn't even thought about it. "Grandmother used to say, 'The only one who knows the future is God. You have to trust Him.'" She smiled at the remembrance. "Trust is easy to say but harder to do... at least for me."

David nodded. "Your grandmother was a wise woman."

"Yes, she was." A tinge of sadness came over Genny as she wished she could be more like her.

David brightened. "Going back to the bowling topic. People do take their bowling seriously here in Worthville. Several bowlers have gone on to national competitions."

Wow, David was an expert on the bowling world in Worthville. "How do you know all this?"

"I bowl."

With that answer, Genny almost fell out of her chair onto Chen's patio.

David laughed. "I'm full of surprises." He winked at

her and picked up the check. "I guess we might as well get to it."

The drive home was quiet but a comfortable quiet like old friends have. When they reached her house, they dove into the boxes with lighter spirits. David lifted a bundle of letters, one fell to the floor, and he retrieved it. "What's this interesting envelope with an insurance company in the return address?" The envelope opened on one end rather than across the back, and he peeled open the flap.

"A premium notice?" Genny moved toward him.

"This isn't the right kind of envelope for a premium notice." He scanned the document in his hand.

Genny pressed against him. "Well?"

At last he turned his eyes to hers. "Forget finding whether the loan was paid off."

"Why? Has something else gone wrong?" A sick fear crept up on her.

He lifted his hand and stroked her face. "Your grandmother must have forgotten about this when we discussed her financial matters. This is a life-insurance policy on her. $25,000."

Genny snatched the policy from his hand. "For real?"

"For absolute real."

Genny jumped around, raised her hands in the air, and squealed. "I get to keep the house; I get to keep the house." Then it felt like the most natural thing in the world to throw her arms around him, and he pulled her close, wrapping her in an embrace. Genny pulled away and peered at him. Her breath caught as his face drew close to hers, but a loud knock on the door interrupted what might have been a kiss.

Genny turned to see Catherine pulling open the screen door and barging into the house, panting. "Sorry to interrupt, but Don returned home from work and said he passed a bad accident on the way home. Looked like Al's truck. The police wouldn't give him any details."

Genny pulled away from David. "I have to go and see if there's anything I can do."

"I'll take you," David said, already moving toward the door.

CHAPTER TWENTY-ONE

G ENNY AND DAVID STOOD BY AL'S bedside in the emergency room. An IV was connected to his right hand and a heart monitor flashed to his left. Al moaned. A drunk driver had run a stop sign and slammed Al's truck so hard, the Jaws of Life were called in to extract him and Lori.

Stitches started in the middle of Al's forehead and curved around his left eye to his cheek. A laceration on his left hand also bore a line of Monocryl sutures. The attending doctor told Genny it took nearly forty stitches to take care of the various gashes on Al's body. His gray hair stuck to his head. He moaned again and then tried to sit up.

"Hey, take it easy. You need to lie still." Genny adjusted Al's pillow for him to lie back. Miraculously, Al hadn't suffered broken bones, but since the impact had been so hard, as a precaution, doctors were doing more tests than usual to make sure he didn't have any hidden injuries. Al would probably need to stay in the hospital at least a day or so.

Al peered at them as if he were looking through a fog. His eyes grew moist. "What happened? My little girl, how is she?"

Genny exchanged glances with David. "Lori is a fighter, Al. She has many good people taking care of her. You rest." Genny tried not to give any more information than necessary.

"She was covered in blood. Is she still alive? Tell me she's still alive. The car hit on her side." A frantic fear rose in his eyes.

Genny patted Al's arm. "She's alive, Al. She's alive."

Al collapsed against the pillow and closed his eyes, exhaling. "Pray for her, okay?"

"Sure, Al, sure. I'll check on you later," Genny whispered. "You try and get some rest."

Al groaned again, apparently too groggy to answer. Genny knew the pain medication he was receiving clouded the brain. She and David exited into the hallway.

David put his hand on Genny's arm. "How is she?"

Genny could say only so much with privacy laws, since Lori wasn't her patient. "While you were parking the car, I asked Lori's nurse if I could speak with the family on Al's behalf. They were about to leave the hospital as Lori was being airlifted to the children's hospital in Atlanta. She's in serious condition. I'll need to check in on Al pretty often with his family gone." Based on what she learned from the family, Lori would need a lot of care to recover, especially since her health had always been fragile.

Genny couldn't believe this turn of events. As the pressure in her life lessened, disaster slammed Al—much worse than what she was dealing with. Losing her house was nothing compared with having a child or grandchild injured. Al was so devoted to Lori too.

David took her elbow. "Are you ready to go?"

She nodded, and they drove home in silence. David didn't say anything else about the insurance policy. He must have seen how trivial it was beside Al's situation. Al had asked her to pray for Lori. It had been so long since she tried. But this was Al asking. She closed her eyes. "God, if You can hear me, please help Lori, and please let me know what I can do to help her."

EARLY THE NEXT MORNING, Genny sat with a cup of coffee on the back steps Al built. The warmth of the cup seeped into her hands. As the sun made its ascent over the horizon, its golden glow bathed the fields behind her house. Up late the night before, she should have slept in, but her eyelids popped open around five o'clock and wouldn't close again. She breathed in the cool morning air—a welcome respite from the ninety-degree temperatures that had dominated the weather in recent times. A bluebird darted from one fence post to another. Butterflies frequented a yellow-and-orange lantana bush beside the steps, and she remembered sitting there as a child, trying to count how many kinds of butterflies came to the bush. Currently pipe-vine swallowtails and eastern tiger swallowtails fluttered on the plant. A squirrel chattered from the oak tree. All appeared right with the world, yet things weren't right.

Not at all.

They'd found the insurance policy. Her problems should have been over, yet they weren't.

She ran her hand along the handrail of the steps. It would take time, but Al would recover. Although she'd called the hospital earlier and tests showed no internal injuries, he was cut, bruised, and had suffered blows in the accident that would have him moving slowly. The stitches would come out soon, and he'd be back on his feet. But how the bruises on his heart healed were directly tied to how Lori progressed.

She faced a long road. The impact crushed her pelvis, which required several pins and plates to reconstruct. She would be bedridden for quite a few weeks, and then she would begin physical therapy. She prayed Lori could avoid getting an infection, which would further complicate matters.

"Anyone here?" a voice called from the house.

"Out back."

Catherine swung open the screen door and plopped onto the steps beside her. "How are you feeling?"

Genny patted Catherine's arm. "I'm okay. Missing Al. Any other time, he'd be here mowing by now." She was beginning to understand her grandmother's feelings toward Lester. Al was family.

"Well, Don sent me over here to tell you he'd be happy to help out in the interim. He's not much of a yardman, but he could keep the grass cut back for a few weeks." Catherine pointed in the direction of her house.

"Have you seen his mower? When we moved out here in the country, he bought a gargantuan thing. He said he didn't want any puny mower if he was going to have to cut two acres." Catherine lowered her voice as if she was about to divulge a secret. "I think he gets a power rush from sitting on it."

Genny laughed. "You tell Don I would appreciate his help." With everything else going on, at least she didn't have to be concerned she'd have a jungle in the yard. If the grass grew up, it could get tricky with the snakes. She didn't mind the king snakes because they kept the rodents down, but she sure didn't want to run up on a copperhead.

Poor Al. At a time in his life when he so anticipated spending more time with Lori, this happened. Lori had come so far. From what she understood from Al, Lori was born to a woman who didn't take care of herself, and she came into the world at a low birth weight. When she was adopted, it took good care to get her close to where other kids her age were. Al said that at six years old, she was still only in the twentieth percentile.

Catherine clapped her hands. "Okay, you can't talk about Al's situation because of privacy laws, but you don't have to. I got my information from his niece at church. So instead, let's talk about this life-insurance policy you found."

The life insurance. She'd told Catherine about it when Catherine called to check on her late the night before. "I don't think it's registered yet. I still don't feel a sense of relief. Maybe it's because of what's happened to Al and Lori. But David says the policy is valid and, with proper documents, it shouldn't take too long to collect on it." Genny needed to collect proof as to her identity, have the papers notarized, and get them to the insurance company as soon as possible.

She should be elated about the insurance, and though she couldn't put her finger on it, the heaviness wouldn't stop.

"You're not too thrilled about this. I mean, you wanted to save your house, and this does it, right?" Catherine extended a hand to her.

Genny took her hand. "Right. I'm sorry. I don't know what's wrong. It's hard to be excited when Al is suffering. His dad was so close to my grandmother."

"It hit her hard when Lester died. He was like a family member." Catherine put her arm around Genny. "I wish there was something I could do."

Genny embraced Catherine. "You are already doing it, my friend."

Catherine stood. "All right, then. I guess I'd better get back to care for the kids while Don does his grass mowing. We'll talk later. And hey, that invitation to church is an open one."

Genny stood as well. "Okay. And thanks."

Catherine walked around the house to go back home, and Genny marveled over how great it was to have a friend like her living right across the street.

The whole time she lived in New York, she never found a friendship as close as this happenstance neighbor. Genny lowered herself to the steps again.

Her phone rang. She plucked it from her pocket and saw it was David. She clicked it on.

"Hi, wondered if you might be up for an out-of-town dinner. I know you're sad about the accident, so it might cheer you. I was thinking Sal's in Atlanta, fine dining, seafood."

She'd heard about Sal's, but she'd never eaten there. "I guess so."

"Tomorrow night?"

She thought a moment. "That's great."

"Pick you up around five to make the trip over."

"I'll be ready." She clicked off the phone just as Elizabeth bobbled around the corner, hopped on the step beside her, and climbed into her lap. Genny found a temporary respite from the emotional weight resting on her as she laughed at her feathered friend. "Well, girl, I love you too." Genny never imagined a chicken could be so affectionate. Did Elizabeth miss her grandmother Agnes?

That familiar ache arose in Genny again, and as she stroked the chicken, she only knew that she sure did. A change of scenery might be nice. David was thoughtful to see that.

CHAPTER TWENTY-TWO

GENNY ADJUSTED THE STRAP OF HER black cocktail dress as David held the door open to Sal's. In their trips into the city, she and her grandmother passed by this restaurant many times, but it was far beyond their budget. That and the fact her grandmother hated seafood eliminated the prospect of them ever eating there. As she entered, she made note of the upscale furnishings and the crisp maître d'.

For sure not Worthville.

After they were seated, the waiter handed them menus, and Genny perused the offerings. The restaurant put her in mind of a seafood place she and Kurt found near Rockefeller Center. They'd stumbled on it one evening while on the way to see a revival of *South Pacific*, near what turned out to be the end of their relationship, right before she found out the truth. She sighed. She needed to quit drawing parallels between her experiences with David and Kurt. It wasn't fair. David helped her save her grandmother's house and spent countless hours doing it. Why couldn't she let go of her apprehension?

David smiled his glorious smile. "Have you decided?"

She put the menu aside. "I think I'll try the swordfish. On the way over, you sold me on it when you told me how good it was."

The waiter suddenly appeared at their table, as if he possessed a listening device to hear their intentions. David ordered her swordfish but then decided on scallops for himself. He directed his gaze toward her. "So you must be feeling relieved."

"I should be." Genny took a sip of water, not really knowing what to say about how she felt.

David raised his eyebrows. "What does 'should' mean?"

Genny shrugged. "I have no idea." She averted her eyes. "I still feel this inexplicable sense of heaviness; for what reason, I don't know."

David grew quiet for a few minutes. "It's all this business about the wreck. How is Al anyway?"

Genny ran her hand over the spotless white tablecloth and smoothed out an invisible wrinkle. The wrinkles in her life were as plentiful as those on a college freshman's T-shirt. No iron in sight. "I spoke with Al today. He insists he's taking over from Don and coming back to work next week, but I don't think it's a good idea." She avoided any details about his medical condition, but she thought Al's voice still sounded weak.

David leaned forward. "I think of Al as the kind of guy who can be pretty determined when he wants to be."

Genny sat tall in her chair. "True. But he needs to take care of himself, and I'm the kind of gal who can be as determined as any man."

David nodded and grinned in that beguiling way of his. "That truth has been made clear to me. It's one of your most outstanding attributes."

Genny studied him a moment. "Not many men think so."

"Well, I do," David said, conviction in his voice. He let his hand rest on hers, and as he did, a tiny spark passed between them. When the moment passed, he said, "With the foreclosure business settled, I think we should go bowling."

Genny laughed. "Really, we're talking about bowling? I don't know about that. Are you any good at it?"

David's chest expanded. "Pretty good at knocking down the pins if I do say so myself."

"How did you ever get into it?" Genny tried to imagine how this man, who hailed from such a highbrow background, would wind up in a bowling league.

David narrowed his eyes in thought. "Worthville is not the entertainment capital of the world, as you already know. So when I moved there, I figured if I was going to be involved in the community, I needed to do what they did. I met a few folks, and almost everybody was going to the bowling alley at least once or twice a week, so I tried it. It's a lot of fun. Haven't you ever bowled?"

The waiter slid their appetizer, shrimp remoulade, onto the table. It smelled heavenly. "In answer to your question, no, I have never bowled. The bowling alley opened during the Worthville renaissance after my departure to points north."

"Well, we could sure use you on our team this fall."

Genny laughed as she pierced one of the shrimp with her fork. It was funny to her that Harriet bowled with college students. She'd misjudged the situation. "What? Do you have people going back to college too like Harriet's team?"

"Nah. High school. Those jocks won't have time to bowl and play football too."

Genny let her fork drop to her plate. "You have football players on your team?"

David smiled as he swallowed one of the shrimp. "You bet. They have so much power, when the ball hits the pins, they about fly through the back wall."

Genny was having to reassess this whole bowling situation. "So why do you need me? I can't do anything like that."

"You don't know what could happen if you try." David's eyes twinkled. "I mean, it might be something great." Once more, he let his fingers rest on her hand.

Genny wasn't sure they were still talking about bowling because this time the spark felt more like a fire. No, she was sure they weren't talking about bowling, and she didn't know what to say next.

She was relieved when the waiter appeared and whisked the appetizer plate away, then served their swordfish and scallops. For a few divine moments,

Genny forgot about insurance policies, Kurt's deviant antics, and even the possibility of being a bowler as she partook of the culinary delights.

THE FOLLOWING TUESDAY NIGHT, Al stood on the front porch with Genny, his shoulders slumped, his head down in dejection. He'd improved physically from his injuries, but his heart was another matter.

She wiped the perspiration from her forehead with the back of her arm and then fanned her T-shirt away from her sticky body. "Are you sure you're ready to mow the grass? I think it's too much for you to be out in this blistering heat. And the humidity is off the charts." Genny checked the weather forecast, and the heat wave from the past week was expected to continue for several days. The push mower from the shed was out in the yard. "And where's your riding mower?"

"Sold it. Lori needs money for medical bills. They ain't got no insurance since her daddy lost his job a few months ago. Pretty desperate situation. She came down with an infection. Needs another surgery, and we don't even know if that's all the surgery she'll need." Al leaned against a porch post, appearing weak. "She's so little. But she's a fighter. Yes, she is."

Elizabeth jumped on the porch and nested on Al's shoe. If Genny were a betting woman, she would've bet Elizabeth was trying to make Al feel better.

Genny put her hands on her hips. "There's no way you're cutting my grass today. Wait a few more days.

Go home."

"But—"

"Go. Doctor's orders."

Al resettled Elizabeth on the porch and turned to move the lawn mower back to the shed.

"Just leave the mower. I'll get it."

Al tipped his hat to her, got in his truck, and left.

He wanted the money to help Lori, yet he'd be risking his health to get it. She needed to figure out a way to help Al and, in turn, help Lori. She scanned the grass, which was growing right before her very eyes. She hated to ask Don to come back over and mow.

Since they found the insurance policy, she didn't have the bad job of going through her grandmother's financial records. She'd mow the grass. Yes, she would. She cranked the lawn mower and set out. It wasn't as if she hadn't done it before. She used to help her grandmother when Lester was overwhelmed with jobs. As she mowed, heaviness continued to haunt her, and then, after she finished the front yard and was heading around back, a thought came to her, and it wouldn't let her go. Was this the answer to the prayer she prayed the day of the accident?

Even the next day, this thought was still with her. As she sat staring into space in her office, her cell phone rang. She took it from her pocket and saw it was David. "Hi."

"Good to hear your voice. When do you expect the money from the insurance company?" David asked.

"I was on the phone with them for an hour this morning. They needed a few more documents, which I have already faxed to the company. After I sign the papers they're overnighting to me and I send them back, I should have the money before the end of the week." She'd made sure they understood the urgency of the matter.

"Your troubles are over, then."

"Right." She tried to feign agreement.

"Genny, what's wrong? You saved the family legacy."

Genny leaned back in her chair. "I have a lot on my mind is all. Can we talk this evening?"

"No problem. If there's anything I can help with, let me know. I'm here. Let's talk after work."

"Sure. Good-bye." She clicked the phone off and put it back in her pocket. "Family legacy," she echoed aloud, remembering Harriet's words. She thought about her grandmother's lifelong struggle and how much it mirrored her challenge.

And she thought about Lori.

CHAPTER TWENTY-THREE

A COUPLE OF HOURS LATER, GENNY exited an exam room and saw David almost marching down the hallway. He'd said they would talk after work, but here he was, and he hadn't called to say he was coming. He motioned toward her office.

"I have to speak with you." He'd never used such a stern tone with her before. It must be his courtroom voice. What was going on?

She turned to Clarice, who was right behind her. "I'll be a moment. You go ahead and get Mr. Winston's vitals."

"No problem. We're not too far behind schedule. Take your time." Clarice slipped into the next exam room.

Genny opened the door to her office. "What is it?"

"Lance just stormed into my office in all of his red-faced glory with that disgusting toothpick in his mouth. He threatened me and told me he heard about the insurance policy and that nothing was going to keep him from building this development. Louvene got so scared, she called the police. He hasn't been over here, has he?"

"No, I haven't seen him." Genny put her hand to her face and shook her head. "I should have called you earlier. I need to tell you something."

They took seats in front of her desk. David looked confused and gestured for her to begin.

Genny inhaled. "I understand the insurance policy seemed like an answer to all of my problems, but…"

"What do you mean 'seemed'? It is an answer to your problems. It is."

He sounded as if he were speaking to her as a client, not a friend, his voice taking on a hard tone. His legal training must gear him up to launch an offensive at unjust situations.

"Al told me his granddaughter needs help with her medical bills. He even sold his mower to help."

David leaned toward Genny, his gaze and his righteous indignation softening. "Sold his mower? Oh my, things must be in desperate straits. I've never seen a man so enamored with a piece of machinery as Al was with his mower."

"Grandmother Agnes always treated Lester and his folks like family, and that's the way they treated her too. I think she'd want me to help Al and little Lori." Genny took a deep breath. "I'm giving them the insurance money. I wouldn't even be able to enjoy my house with Lori needing medical care. Keeping it is not as important as helping Lori. She needs help right now."

David crashed against the back of his chair. "You're

going to lose your house. Wait, why don't you let me help Al and Lori? That way you… "

"No," she interrupted. " This is something I need to do because of what Lester did for my grandmother. So that's that." She folded her hands in her lap.

David shook his head. All the air appeared to go out of him.

"I'm sorry, but I've resolved myself to this."

David shook his head. "Well, all right, then. Given any thought to what you're going to do?"

"I'll go back to New York. I moved here because of the house. Maybe Catherine will take Elizabeth."

"Oh yes, the chicken. Right. Maybe she will." David hung his head for a moment and then stood. "Well, I'll see you. This was an odd turn of events."

Genny walked him out of the office, but neither of them said a word. She believed with all her heart this was the right thing to do, but an overwhelming sadness hung over them like a shroud.

Later in the afternoon, Genny received an urgent call. She went to her office, closed the door, and sat, wondering what medical emergency this might be, but oddly, it was Louvene, David's receptionist. "Dr. Sanders, I hate to bother you, but I just wondered what was going on."

"I don't know what you mean. David told me about Saul Lance and how he stormed into your office." Clarice opened the door, stepped in, and Genny held up a finger to say she'd be with her in a minute. Clarice pointed to her watch and left.

Louvene went on. "Yes, that man had some nerve

showing up like he did. He's a menace, but I don't think that's it. A little while ago, I found David facedown on his desk, right on the third-edition volume of *Georgia Civil Practice*. I told him he had a four o'clock appointment with Sally Herdsman, who wants to sue her neighbor because he's cutting her Red Ruffles azalea hedges when she's not at home. You know if you trim azaleas at the wrong time of year, they won't bloom and—"

Genny interrupted. "Louvene, you were saying about David."

"Yes, sorry. But I have to say I'd want to sue too if somebody cut off my Coral Bells azaleas. Anyway, David lifted his head, got up, and sailed right past me, headed for the front door."

Genny didn't know what to say.

"Dr. Sanders?"

"Yes."

"I've never seen him like that before."

Genny turned over the information in her mind. "You don't know where he went?"

"Not a clue. He's never walked out on an appointment before."

Clarice came back into the office, tapping her watch more emphatically. "Louvene, I have to go. I'll try to give him a call later."

"Thank you, Dr. Sanders."

After they said their good-byes, Genny hung up and Clarice all but pushed her out of the office. "We're forty-five minutes behind schedule," she said. "Edgar Summit has been waiting thirty minutes. You know how grumpy he gets."

She did know. How would she find time to check on David? Where did he go? Was it her news about giving the money away that had him so upset? She didn't know the answers to those questions now, but maybe she would soon. In the meantime, she took a deep breath and braced herself as she opened an exam room door. "Hello, Mr. Summit. It's good to see you."

IN THE EVENING, GENNY tried to clean the mess she and David had made, at least the mess they made going through her grandmother's financial records. There might be a mess in other ways too. An emotional one. She pondered David's reaction to her leaving town and how he'd left his office that day. She'd have to admit it wasn't all about losing the house. It was about losing a relationship. She'd miss David. But what could she do about it? If that thought she had about giving the money to Lori was from God, then what was there to do about David? Maybe she wasn't supposed to be with David. Her heart sank at the idea. If she was completely honest, she wanted to be with him. A lot.

The afternoon temperature soared near one hundred. She'd been thirsty all day, and her medical training taught her that feeling thirst meant she was already dehydrated. She went to the kitchen to refill her tea. She was a Southern gal, and sweet tea flowed through her veins. Her words to Talia Meadows about tea not hydrating like water came back to her, but she craved the dark sweet tea she learned to make like her grandmother's. She was a real hypocrite—criticizing Talia and Harriet about their choices while not living by the advice she gave out. So much sugar. Yet so good.

Nevertheless, she removed the tea pitcher from the refrigerator. When she did, a strange crackling sounded from the backyard. She returned the pitcher, and before she could even step to the kitchen window, a flash illuminated the room. She rushed over to see the shed ablaze against the night sky. She grabbed her cell phone from her jeans pocket and dialed 911. "Yes, fire," she said, trying to retain her composure. "2014 Magnolia Road."

She clicked the phone off and could feel the adrenaline kicking in as she dashed outside. She fumbled to turn on the faucet, yanked on the garden hose, and tried to pull it toward the shed. The fire must have reached some sort of accelerant, maybe the can of gasoline for the lawn mower, because as she managed to get the hose in position, an inferno released inside the structure. Flames shot three stories in the air, making every hair on her body stand on end. She lifted the scant garden hose spray against the raging fire, and its pitiful spurt of water fell on the blaze as the roof collapsed.

As sparks flew high into the night sky, Genny dropped the hose in defeat. The heat of the fire caused perspiration to pour from her face, mixing with the tears that freely fell.

In the rays of first light, Al, Genny, and Catherine gathered around the ruins of the shed. Firemen and an investigator poked around what was left of the outbuilding her grandfather had built decades before. They tried to make sure there were no smoldering embers ready to erupt into flame again.

The destruction of the shed caused the worry lines on Al's face to intensify, and they had already deepened in the weeks since the car accident. "The fire truck sirens wailed last night, but I never dreamed they was comin' to your place. I sure wish I'd been here."

Genny put her hand on Al's shoulder. "You couldn't have done anything. It was too late by the time I found it." Genny thought it amazing she found the blaze at all. If she hadn't refilled her tea, she might have missed it altogether and discovered only ashes the next morning.

"At the hardware store, folks was talkin'." He adjusted his ball cap and shook his head.

"Yes, I guess they were." An abnormal number of cars passed the house all morning as Worthville residents came to see what was going on. Fire was a big deal in Worthville, as the volunteers for the fire department held hero status in the community. They maintained a strong record of being able to save structures, and of course, even though it was a shed, they took it somewhat personally when they lost a building.

One of the firefighters approached her with slumped shoulders. "Sure is a shame about your building. If we'd been here sooner..." He glanced back over to the ruins.

"It was a shed. Not like a house or anything." Genny tried to console him.

"But still. . ." He let his voice trail off and shuffled over to help others stow the fire hose back on the truck.

Genny surveyed the debris in front of her. She'd hoped something could be salvaged, but it appeared all was lost—her grandfather's tools, his fishing equipment including the hand-tied and vintage lures. All gone.

She sighed and turned to Al. "We'd talked about you trying to cut the grass today, but my lawn mower and all my tools burned in that building." She guessed it was just as well she was moving to an apartment. She wouldn't need a lawn mower there. She turned to Catherine. "And you have to go home. I'm fine. You've been here all night."

"Like I was going to lie in my bed with this swarm over here going on. No way. You haven't slept either. Don is working from home today, so we're fine."

How blessed she was to have Catherine as her friend. "I'm glad they got the fire under control." Genny scanned the fields around the house. The recent heat wave left them dry and brittle, as there'd been little rain.

Genny had called Dr. Fleming earlier and told him she'd be late. Thankfully, their appointment schedule was not as heavy as other days. But still, she hated to leave him alone. She hated even more that he was going to have to find someone else so soon. But he couldn't pay her enough to cover the bills Kurt ran up and pay for housing too. She'd have to go someplace where she could make more money.

She scanned the crowd around her, and most of the emergency personnel appeared to be concluding their jobs, winding up hoses, turning off devices, and taking equipment back to trucks. She hoped she'd be back to work within the hour.

Then one of the firefighters began unrolling yellow crime scene tape around the area.

Genny ran to him. "What's going on? Why are you doing this?"

The firefighter pointed toward a man with a notepad in one hand, whose identification tag read, "Fire Investigator." He approached Genny and extended his other hand to her. "Miss Sanders, I'm John Lakeland." She'd hoped he was concluding his investigation and was ready to sign off on the situation, but the yellow crime scene tape sent another message. "I think we have all we need," he declared. "I'm sorry to say it appears to be arson. We'll know more in a few days."

"Arson?" A spike of fear pierced her. "Why would anyone set fire to an old toolshed?"

Lakeland glanced toward the house. "I have no idea, but it's a miracle the fire didn't spread to the house." He looked back over his shoulder to the surrounding land. "Or to your fields. It's been real dry. It could have affected your neighbors."

Genny tried to remain calm, but the fear in her heart threatened to blaze in the same way a few sparks had turned into an inferno the night before. She thought of the family a few hundred yards away. They had a new baby. Catherine told her they were the sweetest folks. She hoped to meet them soon.

Could it be? Was Saul Lance making good on his threats? It was too obvious. He would be at the top of the suspect list. Was he that desperate?

Catherine mumbled something under her breath.

Genny asked, "What did you say?"

"Oh, I was conjecturing on who might have done something so low-down. Here's a clue—the initials are S.L." Genny caught the cynicism in Catherine's voice.

"Yeah, I was wondering too since he made threats when he went to see David yesterday."

Catherine's brows rose. "Threats? You didn't tell me."

Lakeland positioned his pen on a notepad. "Wait a minute. If someone has been making threats, I need to know."

"We thought they were irrelevant because of a new development." There was no way Saul Lance could be aware she was giving the insurance money to Al, though. She hadn't even told Al about it.

Catherine interjected. "New development? You didn't tell me that either."

Al cleared his throat. "I'd like to hear more about this, but I have to get over to my granddaughter's. Her mama has got to go to work, and I need to stay with Lori." Al turned and began walking away.

The fire investigator stepped closer. "Miss Sanders?"

Catherine stopped him. "She has her doctorate. She's Dr. Sanders."

Genny was surprised at how Catherine rushed to set Lakeland straight.

He continued, "Dr. Sanders, then, tell me everything about these threats."

Genny held up a finger. "Could you wait one minute?" She took off after Al, leaving Catherine to converse with the investigator. "Al, stop. I need to speak with you before you go."

She caught him and took his hands in hers. "Al, your family has meant a lot to mine over the years. If it hadn't been for your dad, Grandmother Agnes would have never been able to manage after I left. So when I tell you what I have to tell you, I don't want you to say anything for a minute."

Al shifted on his feet and checked his watch.

He needed to leave, but she didn't want him to go without hearing her out. "I'm giving the money from the insurance policy we found to Lori." Given the circumstances, she had not spoken with Al about the money, but she knew he was aware of it, because Catherine had told his niece, whom he was very close to.

At first, Al froze in place.

"For her medical bills."

Al remained still, almost as if he were in a trance.

Genny shook his hands. "Al, do you understand? For Lori. $25,000 for Lori."

She hadn't anticipated how the news might affect Al.

The next thing he did was pull a big red bandana from his pocket, and she watched a grown man cry. He blubbered for a while and then blew his nose. "I ain't never heard of nothin' so kind in all my life. Why, this is gonna help my little girl get the help she needs, and it's gonna help her mom and dad not worry so much about how they'll pay these medical bills."

"It's the least I can do." Genny would have thought between the heat of the fire and the tears that fell the night before, she would be dehydrated, but she found herself blinking back moisture.

Al glanced at the ruins of the shed. "But you have your problems with the house and the shed. I can't let you do this."

"Al, I don't mean to be rude, but it's not your place to decide. It's my decision and mine alone. I'm giving the money to Lori. I can start over. Your family needs this."

Al wrapped Genny in the biggest hug. If anything good came out of the last twenty-four hours, that embrace was it.

CHAPTER TWENTY-FOUR

DAVID PULLED INTO GENNY'S YARD AND exited his car. He stood a moment, studying the sight of the fire personnel, the crime scene tape, and the smoldering ashes. He approached Genny, arms extended.

"Thanks for coming." She welcomed his arms around her and wrapped hers around his waist, leaning into him.

"I'm so sorry," he said. "I can still hear Saul Lance telling me nothing was going to stop him. I bet you he was the one who set fire to this shed, but how are we going to prove it?" He paused, pulled away, and looked into her eyes. "I hate this. Lance did everything but tell me the exact time he would strike the match."

"It's not your fault. It's going to be a total loss, but at least it didn't spread to the house." She patted his shoulder, trying to console him.

"The house? Could that have been Lance's original intent?" David shook his head as if trying to shake off

191

the horrible thought. "Well, at least you should receive something from the insurance."

Genny looked away.

"Tell me you have insurance."

"Grandmother didn't have any because the house was paid for. I was going to get some, but I kept delaying. There was so much to do with the move, and then all of this with the foreclosure."

He studied her a moment. His eyes bored into her. She felt like a defendant on the stand and he was the prosecutor.

A frown edged across her brow. "Don't look at me that way." His gaze remained unchanged. "I'm not the only one who's made poor decisions. At least I didn't have the bad judgment to take on Saul Lance as a client."

David turned and moved to his car, shoulders slumped. Regret washed over her. Why did her default setting always have to be doubt and suspicion of David harboring some evil plot? She moved toward the car, but he was already pulling out of her driveway.

GENNY TRIED TO JOT a few notes about Harriet's visit, but she found herself scratching out words and rewriting. Probably the lack of sleep. Dr. Fleming said to take the day off, but she knew he was jammed with patients that day. She couldn't keep a train of thought going.

She could feel Harriet's gaze on her and thought everyone in Worthville knew about the shed, since word had gotten out that it was a suspected arson. Harriet didn't say anything, but Genny found it harder and harder to push back the tears, which were about to spill their borders. *Game face. Professional demeanor.* But one single tear began its track down her cheek.

Harriet touched her arm. "What's going on, hon? Why don't you tell me about it? I'll be a stand-in for Agnes."

Genny struggled with letting her guard down in a professional setting. But wasn't her relationship with Harriet more than a professional one since she was close to her grandmother? "I guess it's everything—the shed burning, grandmother's house in foreclosure, and last night, I lashed out at someone I care about."

Genny wiped her eyes with the back of her hand. "I hurt him, and I can't stop thinking about someone who hurt me too. It's so crazy." When would she ever get over her haunting suspicions? She'd never forget the look on David's face when she sliced him with her remark about Saul Lance. He hadn't even said anything about the insurance. She'd just assumed he was judging her.

Harriet eased from the exam table and gave Genny a hug. "Hurting people hurt people. But first things first, honey." Harriet took a lace-edged handkerchief from her pocket and offered it to Genny.

Genny stared at it a moment. The lace appeared to have been handmade. It was almost too beautiful to use, but she dabbed her eyes anyway, not wanting to reject Harriet's offer.

Harriet fixed her gaze right on her. "Remember what I said about the legacy? You think about what your grandmother went through."

Genny nodded. It was a lot to forgive, someone stealing your inheritance right out from under you.

"After you think about it a good long time, it'll come to you what you need to do."

Were Connie and Harriet related? They both possessed the uncanny ability to see what was going on in her heart.

She left work that day knowing what she had to do. She sat in the parking lot behind the office and pulled her cell phone out. When he answered, she didn't hesitate. "I'm sorry. I was wrong to lose it like that. I'd been up all night, but that's really no excuse for how I treated you."

"I'm sorry too," he answered.

"But you didn't do anything."

"I could have been more understanding."

She thought he was pretty understanding already. His capacity to forgive her pettiness was beyond comprehension, considering how nasty she'd been that morning. Relief washed over her, and she breathed deeper, grateful she didn't have to carry that load of guilt a minute longer.

"So in case there's one more thing that could make a difference in the eroding circumstances, let's filter through what remains in the stacks," he said.

"We're on," she said. When he arrived at her house, she placed her hand on his arm. "David, I want to tell you again how sorry I am about this morning."

He nodded. "I didn't mean to be so judgmental."

Genny removed her hand and extended it to him.

"You weren't. It was me. Friends?"

"Friends." When he took her hand, he held it for a few seconds longer than she might have expected for a regular handshake, and for a moment, she wondered whether he might pull her to him. But somehow the moment passed, and she turned to consider what remained for them to examine.

"I have a sinking feeling we're not going to find anything here," she said.

David nodded in agreement. "I have to admit, it's not looking too good." He sat in a dining room chair. "You know, my dad's words have rung in my ears lately. I've been wondering if he was right. I keep thinking a real lawyer would have found an answer in all of this."

She sat in a chair beside him. "You did find an answer, but I chose to go in another direction. Please don't think that way. You are a real lawyer."

He patted her hand. "Thanks. So are you still planning on returning to New York?"

"The person who took my job has given their notice, so I could have it back if I want it. Turns out they weren't cut out for life in the big city." She surveyed the house. "I'll sure miss this place. It breaks my heart to think about it being torn down, having to let go of something so close to my heart." She tried not to make eye contact with David. She had to ask herself whether she was talking about just the house or something else as well.

David remained quiet.

She wished he would say something. Anything.

Genny moved on. "I made contact with Wiersbe's auction house, and they never did business with an Agnes Sanders. Another dead end."

"I hate to tell you, but the stamp expert contacted me too. With the exception of a couple, the stamps were quite common. The two he was interested in would bring a couple hundred dollars at most, and that would take time."

"Thank you for trying. You've done everything you could."

She wondered why she ever came back to Worthville in the first place only to lose everything again. And she meant everything.

She stood and returned to the bundles of paper in front of her. She selected what appeared to be a letter from the top of the stack. Judging from the date, it was written when her grandfather was still alive and was addressed to him. When she opened it, she found it was from Jake Boyle, the mysterious person from whom her grandfather borrowed money. She waved it at David. "Look at this."

He rose and stepped over to see what was in her hand. She wondered whether her grandmother had seen this. In it, Boyle told her grandfather not to worry about the money—he could take as long as he needed to pay it off. He understood family matters. He hoped the money would help his son buy the house he wanted. *Wait. His son meant her father.*

David pointed to something in the letter ahead of where she was reading. She guessed he was so used to scanning documents, his gaze flew over printed material. "Your grandfather's farm didn't do well that year because of a drought, and your father needed money to buy a house, so he borrowed from Jake Boyle against this house."

Her dad must have used the money to buy the place she lived in when she was little. When her dad died, they sold the house and moved in with her grandmother, who told her the money from the sale was put into her college fund.

So the money borrowed from Jake Boyle helped Genny get her doctorate. Somehow it didn't come as a surprise her grandfather put his house at risk to help her dad buy one—something her grandmother, the most giving person she'd ever known, would have done. Her grandfather must have been like her.

She handed the letter to David, who scanned the rest of it. "Your grandfather borrowed the money, and then almost immediately he and Jake Boyle died. Then your father died, so no one was aware of the loan."

Genny shook her head. "I guess not; evidently, not even my mom. Well, at least that mystery doesn't have to be unraveled anymore."

They plunged into the task before them, trying to keep the conversation light. They discussed Harriet's bowling ambition, Connie's magical effect on children, and the renaissance of Worthville. But the longer they spent scanning old utility bills, grocery receipts and accumulating still more recipes, reality confirming the growing resignation in Genny's heart.

She would lose the house.

CHAPTER TWENTY-FIVE

After David left, Genny sat in the swing, staring into the setting sun. She wanted to remember the beauty of this moment when she returned to New York. The city was beautiful too but not like this—the stillness of a summer evening, a whippoorwill calling from a nearby tree branch, Elizabeth nesting on the seat beside her.

She stroked the chicken's back. She'd spoken to Catherine about taking her, and she'd agreed. If she could have chosen anyone to take the fowl, it would be Catherine, but having Elizabeth was like having a little of her grandmother still here. It would be hard to leave the chicken behind. Genny's cell phone rang, and she pulled it from her pocket.

The caller ID was the local hospital. She answered.

"Dr. Sanders, this is Nurse Rita at Worthville General. Sorry to interrupt your evening, but your patient, Harriet Glaussen, came into the emergency room with extremely high blood pressure a few minutes ago."

"Oh yes. I'll be right there." Genny said good-bye, hung up, and went to make herself as presentable as possible without taking too much time. She tried not to speed on the way to the hospital. She knew she was not to become emotionally involved with her patients, but she feared that ship had already sailed with Harriet. The connection to her grandmother was too strong, and she felt a special bond with this unique woman. When she arrived, a heavy weight descended on her when she found a pale Harriet lying in a bed in the emergency room.

She blinked at Genny. "Who called you?"

"The hospital, of course. Besides the fact I've been caring for you on a regular basis, you were friends with my grandmother."

Harriet tried to sit. "You mean you're not my friend?" She was not without an element of her usual spunk.

Genny laughed. "Of course I am." She leaned toward Harriet. "You need to lie back." Genny adjusted her pillow for her. "So how are you?"

"Okay for a woman who was within two pins of beating Gladiola Spears." Harriet moved her arm in a circle. "I don't know if I'm sore from hitting the floor or so much bowling." She let her arm collapse by her side. "Anyway, I got a spare in the final frame and needed five more pins in the next roll. Then I felt a little dizzy, lost my balance, and wound up staring at the ceiling." Harriet narrowed her eyes. "If I didn't know better, I'd think Gladiola spiked my juice."

Genny laughed again but then grew more pensive as she scanned Harriet's chart. "The good news is you didn't break anything, but I still can't understand why this happened. You were doing so much better."

Harriet dropped her gaze and grew sheepish.

"Oh no. You ate cheese crunchies, didn't you?"

Harriet narrowed her eyes, her jaw tightening as she became defiant. "I told you they're my game food."

A creeping despair set in. Again. "Unless you want more of this, change your game food to carrots."

Harriet turned up her lip, exasperated.

Genny sighed. "I'd better go and let you rest. Dr. Fleming and I are going to release you, but we want you in the office first thing tomorrow."

"Oh, yippee," Harriet said, feigning excitement.

Genny turned to go, but Harriet touched her arm. "Don't forget to forgive."

Again, how could Harriet tell she was struggling? But this was no time to ask.

"None of us knows when we might find ourselves spread-eagle in a bowling alley, lights out for good. Of course, I'm not worried about going to glory. I'm ready to meet the Almighty anytime. We are on good terms."

Genny nodded, marveling at Harriet's peace, and then turned to leave.

In a half hour, when Genny arrived home, she changed into her pajamas and decided to sort through the last stack of receipts from her grandmother. She was almost through living in this time capsule. As hard as it was, these boxes contained insight into her grandmother's life, what she valued and loved. Genny found her grandmother always gave 10 percent of her income to the church. For sure, that couldn't have been easy. Beyond that, she'd found she also gave to a food ministry for the poor, a missionary in Ghana, and one of her favorite places to send money was the Gideon ministry, which placed Bibles all over the world.

She'd learned her grandmother would rather order used books online than spend money on a new sofa. Genny looked around at the stacks of books in every corner and the poor old frayed sofa that had been around since she was little. Her grandmother didn't just collect books; she read them. Lots and lots of mysteries.

She'd found a few eccentricities, like the catalog with the electric manicure set. Her grandmother loved gadgets, which was further confirmed by a receipt for a door chime that sounded like a rooster crowing. Genny had been grateful it was never installed when she found it in a kitchen cabinet.

Genny came to a bundle secured by an old rubber band that popped when she tried to remove it. A drawer in the kitchen was set aside for letter, bills, recipes, and other odds and ends. As they'd gone through all the boxes, it looked like she'd wait until the drawer became full and would then take everything out, put a rubber band around it, and throw it in one of the boxes. As Genny sifted through this stack, she found an envelope that made her pause. There was one word written on the envelope, and it was in her grandmother's handwriting—*Bert*. She frowned and opened it.

She read aloud. "Dear Bert, it's been years since you died, but I still think about you every day. I was always angry with you even though I tried to be the good woman everyone thought I was. For so long, I didn't realize how I'd been holding on to the unforgiveness. It took a long time for me to understand how much I hated you, my brother. I lived with the feelings for you so long, I erroneously came to accept them as part of my life."

Genny glanced at the top of the page. The date indicated the letter was written over ten years before, about the time she'd gone off to school. Maybe being left alone with her thoughts caused her grandmother to deal with her feelings for her brother at last. She flipped to another page.

"I'm tired of hating, tired of going over all you took from me. I've had more than any one person could even dream—a husband that loved me, a precious son who gave me a daughter-in-law, and a granddaughter I love more than life itself."

Genny smiled and blinked away the moisture in her eyes.

"I won't let unforgiveness steal one more second of my life. I'm asking God to help me forgive you once and for all and release this awful bitterness. I declare I love you, and somehow, I think you know. Love, Agnes."

Genny dropped the letter, pulled a tissue from her pajama pocket, and bawled.

THE NEXT TUESDAY NIGHT, Harriet Glaussen turned in her seat and winked at Genny as someone hit a strike in the lane next to hers. Genny glanced over to see who it was, and Gladiola Spears sauntered back to her seat. Harriet Glaussen and Gladiola Spears were the last bowlers left standing, and their scores were almost tied. One would have the lead for a moment, and then the other would grab it.

Harriet crossed her eyes and turned back around. Genny grabbed her stomach in laughter. How in the world did Harriet get back on her feet so fast after the last hospital incident? Over the course of two days, players from the Worthville Weasels, the Worthville Wolves, and the Worthville Woodchucks battled it out. Bowler after bowler fell. High school football jocks left in ruins. College basketball players stumbled and fell. Many citizens of Worthville brushed away a tear as their final scores were tallied, all defeated by two champions disguised as geriatric women.

David, eliminated about halfway through, joined her to watch the two duke it out.

Genny leaned over to him. "Is there a bowling channel?"

He frowned at her. "Bowling channel?"

"Right, cause if there is, this should be on it. Have you ever seen anything like it?" Why, the comedy alone was worthy of a reality TV show, not to mention the athleticism. Cheese crunchies notwithstanding, these women ought to teach classes for senior citizens on how to get moving. Every time Gladiola would excel, Harriet would make some sort of face. When Harriet would pull ahead, Gladiola would make a crazy gesture. If this didn't turn out well, maybe Harriet would need to revisit the forgiveness lecture she gave her.

Half the time, the audience was overwrought with hysterics because of their antics.

Harriet pulled off what David called a chicken, and then Gladiola came back with a chicken sandwich. No idea what it was, but David said it was good.

Whatever it was made Harriet fume. On her turn, she picked up a ball and let it go with such force, Genny thought she was going to make a depression in the back wall.

"Did you see that?" Genny asked David, wide-eyed.

He shook his head, incredulous. "Strike," David called as the ball hit the pins and sent them flying in all directions.

The audience roared.

Harriet pivoted and gave Gladiola a sassy look. The crowd went wild with laughter.

After several minutes, the two were neck and neck, and neither could gain a lead as they approached the final frames.

The crowd in Bodine's Bowling Alley went silent. "This will be the last frame," David whispered.

Genny held her breath as Harriet picked up the ball and took a deep breath.

She approached the pins, took a step, and let go.

CHAPTER TWENTY-SIX

TWO DAYS LATER, ON THURSDAY, BEFORE the doors opened at Dr. Fleming's, Genny emerged from her office to a group of nurses gathered around a newspaper.

Genny joined them. "What's going on? It's almost time to see patients."

They held the newspaper for her to see. "It *is* one of our patients."

The front page of the *Worthville Weekly* featured a photo of Harriet smiling big, holding a bowling trophy. Gladiola, last year's champion, still held on to the trophy in what Genny remembered as something of a tug-of-war before she finally let go. Gladiola was not smiling in the picture. The headline read, "Worthville Woodchuck Glaussen Gleans Trophy from Gladiola." Genny took the paper and smiled at the over-the-top alliteration.

"Well, you did it, Harriet. Good for you." Genny recalled seeing Harriet jump a good twelve inches in the air after she hit the final strike. She'd never forget

Gladiola Spears standing there with her hands on her hips, defeated.

Again, she marveled at how this woman rose from a hospital bed to come back and take the trophy. She guessed she did it by sheer will. As she handed the paper back to the nurses, she hoped against hope Harriet hadn't done it high on cheese crunchies. She didn't see her eat any, but she could have loaded up before the competition.

Around eight that evening, Genny went through stacks and stacks of the *Worthville Weekly*.

"Could you hand me more newspaper?" Catherine extended her hands, and Genny filled them with about two months of newspaper editions. Catherine had brought them over from Don's grandmother, who was something of a pack rat and quite reluctant to let go of the newspapers until Catherine told her how desperate Genny was for packing material. "Well, since they're going to a good cause," she'd said.

Genny zipped packing tape across the top of a box to seal it. "It seems you were just helping me unpack boxes."

Catherine nodded. "I *was* just helping you unpack boxes. But, on the other hand, a lot has happened in a short time." Catherine took in her surroundings. "At least you'll have some neat old furniture when you do get your house."

Genny wrapped a dish and put it in a box. "I have no idea when that might be. It's going to take a long time to pull out of my hole of bad credit. Most of this will have to go in storage."

She'd decided to pack almost everything and put it in a pod, which would go to a storage facility. Someday, when she got a place big enough, she could reclaim her items. In the meantime, she would keep what she could take with her in a few suitcases and find a furnished apartment.

"Who do you have helping you move?" Catherine rolled a vase in newspaper.

"Al rounded up a few people. I'd like to have a little more time to sort through Grandmother's things, but I don't. I wouldn't have accomplished as much as I already have if not for searching every crevice of this house." Weariness came over her even thinking about all the times she'd rifled through this house, looking for various things that might rescue it from destruction.

"I guess you'll have to see it this way: if you hadn't come back to Worthville, Lori would have never gotten the money she needed for medical help. She might not have made it without you."

Genny nodded. "Catherine, you always have a way of putting a positive spin on things."

"I try." Catherine taped another box shut. "Don will be at home, so I can help on moving day." Catherine extended a hand to Genny, and Genny placed her hand on top of Catherine's.

Catherine said, "For some reason, I feel like everything is going to be okay."

She smiled at Catherine's optimism in what she hoped was not a patronizing way.

After Catherine left, Genny thought about Catherine's words and questioned whether anything would ever be okay. The road ahead appeared to hold more of what she'd left behind.

She put a stack of books in a box, among them her grandmother's old Bible. Seeing it brought back wonderful memories and something else she couldn't put a finger on. It's as if she wanted to put the Bible in the carton as fast as she could so she wouldn't have to see what was inside. Was she afraid of what it might say to her? The last thing she wanted was to live her life in fear, so she cracked it open. It fell to a passage in Ephesians 4, which her grandmother had highlighted and underlined as if she read it many, many times.

"Be kind and compassionate to one another, forgiving each other, just as in Christ God forgave you." These words bored into her soul with a challenge.

AL'S TRUCK PULLED INTO the yard on Saturday morning as Catherine and Genny stood on the porch. From the truck spilled Al and two men wearing matching white jumpsuits.

They all stomped onto the porch, and Al gestured toward his cohorts. "These here are my two brothers, Chester and Troy. They've got a painting business, but they're off today, so they said they'd pitch in."

Genny extended her hand to each of them. "Thank you so much."

The brother Al identified as Chester spoke first. "We're happy to help Mrs. Agnes's granddaughter. She sure was special to our daddy." Chester's eyes took on a glossy sheen.

Troy echoed his brother's sentiments. "Yes, ma'am, Mrs. Agnes was something else."

Genny appreciated the accolades about her grandmother and held the door open for everybody. "Well, as you can see, the container was delivered this morning, and we can start loading." Genny gestured to the large white pod sitting in front of Grandmother's car. "They'll come back and get it tomorrow. Please come in. We'll start upstairs. I'm hoping we can get this all done today." They filed in, Catherine first, followed by the men.

When they gathered at the top of the stairs on the second story, Genny gave instructions. She'd been thinking about the most time-effective way to move everything. "Troy, why don't you and Chester start in the guest bedroom while the rest of us empty this one." She pointed to her bedroom. "David is coming in a while, and he can help whoever needs him."

With all David's previous help, she rejected his offer to help her move, but he was undeterred. He'd said he would be there as soon as he got another project started. She wondered what he might be doing on a Saturday morning so early, but she didn't want to pry. Well, she did, but nosiness must be put on the back burner with so much to do.

Troy and Chester shuffled off to work. Al hoisted a nightstand and carted it out while Genny and Catherine stripped the bed and lugged the mattress—which bore the scar of when she opened it, looking for cash—down the stairs.

A vain effort.

After everyone returned to the bedroom, they removed the bottom drawers from a tall armoire and stacked them against the wall. Then, with Genny and Catherine on one side and Al on the other, they intended to tilt the armoire on its side and carry it downstairs. Yet when they tried, it wouldn't budge.

Al frowned and called out, "Hey, Troy, Chester. Can you come in here?" They needed more power. After all, it was one big piece of furniture.

The men came in and put muscle into lifting the armoire. Immovable.

"I ain't never seen nothing like it. It's like it's nailed to the wall." When he said it, they all looked at one another and then moved to check behind the armoire.

"Mighty strange. On this side, it appears somebody's put hinges on the back to anchor it to the wall," Al said.

Genny moved to where Al stood. "Let me see." Sure enough, metal hinges were affixed to the back of the armoire. She never even thought to look back there, which was surprising given all the other places she looked in this house. She must have passed by it because of its proximity to the wall and having no room to hide anything. "Why would anyone do that?"

Al rubbed his scruffy beard. "I don't have any idea, but it makes the chest sort of like a door. And look here." Al pointed to the base of the armoire. "There are rollers on the bottom."

"Well, let's open it," Genny declared.

They pulled back the rug and arcing marks scarred

the floor from the armoire having moved across it. "I declare." Al squatted to examine the marks. "This chest has been moved I don't know how many times."

His brother Chester joined him and stroked the marks. "So many times, the rollers have left grooves."

They all exchanged glances, and Al gave the armoire the slightest tug. Like magic, it easily swung away from the wall, light as a feather.

Behind the chest was a small door.

CHAPTER TWENTY-SEVEN

ENNY, CATHERINE, AL, CHESTER, AND TROY froze, glancing first at one another, then at the door.

Amazed, Genny said, "This was not here when I was little. It couldn't have been." She tried the door and found it locked.

Al peered around the edges of the doorframe. "No, ma'am. This door wasn't here then. This here door has been cut in recent times. Within the last decade at least. I believe this might be Dad's work."

Catherine moved in closer. "What do you think is behind it? Maybe behind this door is another space-time continuum. We could walk through it and be jesters in King Arthur's court or maybe into the future and become the first people to live on Mars."

Genny wondered whether Catherine needed to spend a wee bit more time with adults.

Al pointed to the lock. "See how shiny the lock is. It's new too—only a few years old." He peered at Genny. "You know where the key might be?"

Genny smiled, remembering. "I sure do."

She raced downstairs and came back carrying the key with the red ribbon. She put the key in the lock, turned it, heard the click, and pushed open the door. Genny stepped inside as the others followed. The sight before her took her breath away.

Light streamed in two windows on dozens and dozens of canvases. "Oh my!" Genny exclaimed.

"Have you ever?" Al said.

Catherine held her hands over her mouth.

Chester and Troy were wide eyed.

When Genny regained enough of her senses to move, she stepped to one of the canvases. It depicted the Worthville Main Street in the evening with all the flickering lights of the stores. She lingered over it a moment, trying to imagine her grandmother out snapping photos after dark. Or did she paint this from memory? The next painting was of the Worthville depot but from a perspective she'd never seen painted on canvas. She moved on to another, which showed the old feed store where David's office was located. Still another depicted the turn-of-the-century church of which her grandmother had been a lifetime member.

There were several portraits of Elizabeth the chicken with a crown on her head. A royal old bird indeed. As Genny continued to look, she found a portrait of the chicken that preceded Elizabeth, named Audrey, and the chicken before that, named Kathleen. Even the first chicken her grandmother named Barbra for Barbra Streisand. Definitely a diva, her grandmother had said when she'd first brought her home.

The paintings stood stacked six and seven deep and surrounded the attic, which her grandmother had converted into a studio. All this time, Genny thought the space inaccessible. Without her even realizing it, tears had tracked down her cheeks at the wonder of this discovery.

With her sleeve, she swiped her cheeks and brow in the unventilated attic. She opened a window on the front side of the house to get some air moving. "How did Grandmother stand the heat to paint?" Genny asked of no one in particular.

Al removed a wooden panel from the back window and pointed to a contraption on the floor. "I believe your grandmother must have bought this here air conditioner." He picked a floppy hose off the floor and inserted the end, adapted to fit in the space of the panel he'd removed from the window. "Dad must have rigged this. See, you put this hose here..." He reached over and plugged in the unit. "Then you turn it on." The air conditioner hummed to life. "And you got yourself a nice cool temperature." Al pointed to exposed rafters with shiny insulation between them. "Dad must have rolled this insulation to help keep the cool air in."

Welcome air emanated from the unit. From the outside, the attic window showed a pane replaced with wood, but she thought it was a temporary fix for a broken windowpane put there atop a ladder, confident there was no access from the inside. She never guessed someone replaced the glass with wood to use an air conditioner.

Al took hold of another electrical cord. "This here's

for the winter. An electric heater."

Lester and her grandmother had thought of everything.

She took a deep breath and moved into the rest of their discovery. Jars of well-used brushes and trays of oil paints filled tables, while an easel was placed in a north-facing window, the very best kind of light for painting, her artist friend had told her.

There were landscapes of the countryside around the farmhouse in addition to paintings she'd captured of Connie's Coffee and Cones, Harry's Hardware, Chen's Chinese. In fact, almost every local landmark and business was documented in this attic. To her knowledge, no one had ever painted Worthville in this scope before.

Genny turned to the slack-jawed crowd around her. "I can't believe this. She must have done these in the ten years I was away."

Genny spotted an envelope on the table with her name on it. She paused, not knowing what it might hold. Was she ready to see it? While the others inspected the paintings, she peeled back the flap.

"Dear Genny, if you're reading this, I guess I've gone on, and you've solved the puzzle and found what your crazy grandmother did these past few years. You know I love a good mystery, and I anticipated you wouldn't be able to forget about the red ribbon on the key or the other clues like the paintbrushes in the cabinet and the frames in the shed. I thought it might serve as a distraction to missing me as I would miss you. I didn't need a lock on the door to the attic but couldn't resist the opportunity to have a little fun. (Didn't you think that *Art in Georgia* book was a nice touch?) I knew I wasn't going to live forever, so I set things up a while ago. I don't know what you'll do with these paintings, but they're yours. I once thought about selling them but decided against it. Maybe you can hang them in the fields and use them as scarecrows."

Genny laughed and cried at the same time.

"Save one picture of Elizabeth, the royal old bird. Hope you have as much fun in your old age as I have in mine. Don't grieve too much, but live your life to the fullest. When I forgave Bert, it caused me to see the world again, and I was compelled to paint the beauty."

Genny surveyed the paintings and then turned back to the letter.

"The one key missing from my box was the key of forgiveness. These words in Ephesians 4 changed my life: 'Be kind and compassionate to one another, forgiving each other, just as in Christ God forgave you.' When I could stand the bitterness no longer, I surrendered it to God, and He took it and in exchange gave me joy. I am so glad I didn't miss out on all God had for me."

Genny turned full circle, awestruck, taking in the paintings around her—a display spilled from the deep work in her grandmother's heart. Then it hit her what this discovery meant. She'd been wrong in her reaction when Harriet told her about the legacy her grandmother left her. Yes, very wrong. A legacy of forgiveness could stop a foreclosure after all.

She pulled her cell phone from her pocket and

punched a name that was now listed in her favorites. "You have to get over here."

In a short time, she heard his voice. "Genny, are you in here?"

"In here."

"In where?"

Genny popped out through the armoire.

"What is this, a C. S. Lewis book or something? Where did you come from, Narnia?" David asked when he spotted her.

Genny laughed. "No, but someplace as magical. Come with me."

David followed her behind the armoire, stepped through the door, and then froze.

"It's what my grandmother did while I was gone." Genny smiled and pointed to the door through which they'd come. "Lester must have cut the door, because she told me when I was little that there was no access to this attic and the dormer windows were to balance the outside." Genny shrugged. "I guess she tired of the space being wasted, so she turned it into her secret studio."

"I can't believe this...wait, this could be...this could be the answer. You could sell them."

Genny scanned the attic's contents. "I'd already considered these paintings may be Grandmother's last gift to me and will keep Saul Lance from taking this house."

David moved in front of the feed store painting. "I think I know someone who would pay top dollar for this one. It would look great in my reception area." He laughed and then noticed something in a corner. He moved toward a stack of paintings and pulled out one whose edge alone had been visible. He held it, clearly deeply moved by the depiction.

"David, what is it?" Genny stepped to his side to see. "Oh my. I guess she didn't forget."

"This is a treasure." He studied the rendering of the old Worth mill. "I can't believe she went all the way out there to paint this. And she didn't get stuck."

Genny laughed with him as they recalled their day hiking from the mill. "Not that we know of anyway."

David leaned the painting back against the wall. "Everyone in Worthville will be clamoring to get these. Their sale will more than cover paying off the security deed."

Genny's brow furrowed. "So how will this work? It's going to take time to sell these paintings."

David thought a moment. "Lance can't take possession until after the first Tuesday of the month, when foreclosures take place. That would be August 7. We'll file an action as soon as we can on Monday."

"Action?" Genny folded her arms, waiting for David to answer.

"I forget the general population doesn't understand the lingo. Same thing for me if you talked shop. I wouldn't understand a quarter of what you said. It means to get a judge to issue an injunction. It may be a long shot, but it's worth a try. We may stop Lance yet."

She nodded. Maybe she wouldn't have to leave after all. She edged closer to David, hope rising in her. For a while, they both stood silent in the studio, taking in the enormity of the discovery, hearing Catherine, Chester, Al, or Troy ooh and ahh at their first sight of every painting.

He slipped his arm around her shoulders. She intertwined her fingers with his. Finding these paintings could change everything. She glanced up at David. Yes, everything. Her heart soared at the possibilities.

CHAPTER TWENTY-EIGHT

G ENNY ENCOURAGED AL AND HIS FAMILY to pick
out their paintings. After all, in many ways,
Lester helped her grandmother do this. She
thought Harriet should also be one of the first ones to
see the paintings and to select one, so she gave her a call.

Harriet came right over, wearing her Worthville
Woodchucks Bowling Champion T-shirt.

When Genny showed her the room, she about
fainted. Genny thought she might have to put on her
professional cap for a moment. "I can't believe I didn't
know about this. Me, her best friend and all. Agnes sure
could be clandestine."

Genny told her how her grandmother left the
mystery of the key with the red ribbon.

"Sounds like Agnes. She sure did like a good puzzle
to solve. I guess she thought you'd like one too."

Harriet dug around until she found the painting she
wanted most. Her grandmother ignored no vistas in
Worthville. She'd depicted Bodine's Bowling Alley from

several vantage points. Harriet selected the one painted from the right side. "It has a clearer view of the parking spot I always use," she said.

Genny sent Al and his crew home since she didn't know whether the move was still on. David was off to work on stopping it from his angle. He said he thought of an idea he didn't want to share until he'd researched it. She guessed he didn't want to get her hopes up unless he thought it stood a reasonable chance of helping.

She took a rag and ran it over a painting. Several months of accumulated dust stuck to the cloth. Genny scanned how many she needed to dust and grew a bit overwhelmed at the job. Even after Harriet selected her painting, she continued to poke around, and after about half an hour, she came over to Genny. "Well, I've counted. There appears to be seventy-one paintings, even after the ones we've all selected."

Seventy-one. She hadn't imagined there were so many. Her grandmother was quite prolific. Harriet held one of the paintings of Elizabeth. "If you don't mind, I'd like to buy this one as well. I'm thinking this could be a portrait of me too. She always said I was a bird. It'll work real well beside my bowling champion trophy." Harriet laughed but then grew sterner. "I'm not taking these paintings as a gift. I insist on paying or I won't have them at all. I believe Agnes would have wanted me to help her granddaughter anyway I could. Besides, what else am I going to do with my money? I can't take it with me." Harriet inspected the portrait again. "I can't wait to call Gladiola and tell her about this. She's going to want to buy a painting too."

Genny couldn't believe her ears. "You're friends with Gladiola?"

Harriet squinted and pursed her lips at her question. "Well, of course. I was a bridesmaid at her wedding fifty years ago. Because we're a little competitive doesn't mean we aren't friends. She's the reason we moved to Worthville."

Genny shook her head. Harriet was a well of never-ending surprises. "You learn something every day."

JUDGE STEPHENS'S CHAMBERS WERE even more imposing than Genny imagined they might be. The walnut-paneled walls, the leather-bound law books lining the shelves, and his almost museum-quality desk made her feel the same way she did when, as a high schooler, she'd stared at the Lincoln Memorial in Washington—kind of small. She and David sat across from his empty chair late on Monday afternoon, waiting for him to finish in the courtroom. Dr. Fleming had let her go a little early so she could take care of this. She didn't know what Judge Stephens looked like, but she anticipated he'd be graying at the temples and quite stern.

When the door opened, she wasn't sure who the young man with a scruffy hairstyle was. David jumped from his seat. "Judge Stephens, it's good to see you." They shook hands in a vigorous way.

"You too, David. How's Louvene? I bet she's keeping you straight."

David laughed. "She sure tries. I think I'm an

impossible case."

Judge Stephens smiled and sat. "I might be inclined to agree." He moved a few files around on his desk. "So what do you have for me today?"

Genny was still trying to process that this man, who appeared to be a few years out of law school, was a judge. She guessed this was what some folks went through when they came to her instead of their beloved Dr. Fleming. Maybe they thought she too wasn't old enough to have the wisdom to take care of them, and here she was experiencing the same thing in her apprehension about Judge Stephens. This lighthearted man contrasted with the import of his surroundings.

David handed him a file of photographs. "Judge, like I told you on the phone, this place is a treasure trove. The house should be given protective status because it's the home of what's soon to be Worthville's most renowned artist."

Genny sat a little straighter in her chair, listening to David's accolades about her grandmother.

Judge Stephens studied the photographs in the file. "Prolific too." He grinned. "She used to babysit my kids when they were little. They'll tell the stories she told them to my future grandchildren. They loved Agnes and her tales." Judge Stephens started to chuckle. "There was this one about groundhogs with some sort of insects in their burrow."

Genny smiled. "Termites?"

Judge Stephens hit his desk with his hand. "That one cracks me up."

David and Genny exchanged smiles.

David continued. "With the sale of the paintings, I think Genny could pay off the security deed and save the house from destruction."

Judge Stephens handed the photos back to David. "I'll issue a temporary injunction to stop Lance's foreclosure."

Genny grabbed David's hand and squeezed. "Thank you, Judge Stephens. This means so much to me."

Judge Stephens nodded. "Agnes meant a lot to us." He smiled, stood, and shook David's and Genny's hands, then exited.

On the way home, Genny turned to David. "So do you think this is going to work?"

David grinned as he turned onto her road. "I think we have a genuine miracle on our hands."

Genny's phone rang. She answered.

"Dr. Sanders, Mrs. Glaussen is back in emergency. She's in critical condition."

"Thank you for calling. I'll be right there." She clicked off the phone, heartsick. "We have to get to the hospital. It's Harriet."

David made a U-turn, and in minutes, Genny stood beside Harriet's bed. A ventilator breathed for her—a far cry from the woman who won the bowling tournament a week or so before.

The nurse handed her a chart. "We thought she'd come around like she has so many times before, but this is different."

Genny took a moment to scan the chart. It didn't look good. "An ischemic stroke."

The nurse nodded, her gaze downcast.

She moved to the head of Harriet's bed, stroked her hair, and said, "You hang on, Harriet." She sat in a chair beside the bed. "David, do you mind if I stay awhile?"

He responded by pulling up a chair near her. "I'll stay too."

After a couple of hours, Genny rose to go, and as she did, David wrapped an arm around her. "This is hard. She was so close to your grandmother."

Genny patted David's hand. "True. But she was much more than a patient to me. She was like family." As they passed the nurse in the hallway, Genny said, "Let me know if there's any change."

Together, they headed to the car, and Genny was glad to not be making this walk alone. When they arrived at her house, instead of going inside, Genny turned to David. "Let's sit on the porch awhile."

They took their places on the swing and listened to the crickets chirping as dusk settled. Genny never tired of the contrast between the city of her former residence that never slept and the quiet of rural Georgia. She loved the city in many ways and enjoyed the hustle and bustle of urban life, but she was a country girl at heart.

She let her head rest on David's shoulder and sighed. Harriet's condition concerned her. She'd seen this kind of thing before in other patients. One last goal accomplished, and then the patient checks out. Almost as if he or she says, "I've done it, and I'm going." Harriet was spiritually ready to leave this life as she told her, but Genny didn't know whether she could let her go. She'd become far more involved with this patient than any other she'd cared for.

David interrupted her thoughts. "Lovely this evening." His statement seemed part question, part declaration.

"Lovely." She sighed again. She tried to shift her thoughts. "I hate to interrupt such a tranquil moment, but I need a game plan for what I'm going to do with these paintings."

David sat quiet a moment before answering. "A silent auction maybe?"

Genny nodded. "Right, and I'm thinking out loud here. We could use the depot and contact the historical society too. There are so many depictions of Worthville landmarks. Maybe I could donate a percentage to them for helping sponsor the exhibit."

"Good idea." David ran his hand through his hair. "I think Gladiola Spears is the president."

Genny laughed. "She's a mover and shaker, isn't she?" She grew more serious. "I sure hope to raise enough to clear the debt."

David patted her arm. "Keep the faith. It's going to happen."

Genny's phone buzzed in her pocket. When she pulled it out and saw the caller ID, she clicked it on and somehow knew what the phone call meant. "It's Harriet, isn't it?" she asked without even bothering to say hello.

"Nurse Evans here. Yes. I'm afraid it is. She slipped away a few minutes ago."

"Thank you for letting me know," she said, her voice calm and even. She clicked off the phone and turned to David. She shook her head, her lips beginning to tremble, and then buried her face in his chest.

CHAPTER TWENTY-NINE

A WEEK LATER, ON TUESDAY, AS Genny cleared her desk, she smiled while scanning a familiar chart. She touched it with love and gave it to Clarice. "This is Harriet Glaussen's chart. We'll need to send it to storage."

Clarice nodded and took the chart. "She was often the highlight of my day."

"And mine too."

As Clarice opened the door to exit, Gladiola Spears stood there with her hand in the air about to knock.

"Come in, Mrs. Spears. Dr. Sanders is expecting you."

Genny extended her hand to Gladiola while studying the tight French twist atop her head. How in the world did she get every hair in place? And her makeup—it almost appeared to have been professionally done.

Gone were the bowling shirt and baggy pants, replaced with a suit fit for a first lady and a high-end handbag. Pearls even. What a transformation, a bare resemblance to the woman she'd seen at the bowling alley.

Somehow Genny drew her attention away from Gladiola's appearance and found her words. "I'm Genny Sanders. Pleased to meet you, Mrs. Spears. Harriet spoke of you." She didn't say how Harriet spoke of her. Why did Harriet never mention what a fashion plate Gladiola was? Genny motioned toward a chair in her office. "Won't you have a seat? Thank you for coming on such short notice."

Gladiola eased into a chair, crossed her ankles, and placed her bag in her lap. "Genny? Is that short for Virginia, Genevieve…?"

"Genevieve."

"That's what I'll call you, then. Harriet said you two were close. She was a dear—a fierce bowling competitor, but a dear. Wasn't her service lovely? I miss her in a desperate way, as I know you do."

"A real tribute. The bowling shoes and trophy on display were a nice touch." Harriet's service evoked so much emotion for Genny, and she blinked away the moisture in her eyes at the thought.

Gladiola nodded. "The trophy mementos were my idea. Now, to the matter at hand. I hear we've found our Agnes left a vast collection of paintings. I can't believe she didn't tell me. We worked together on several committees at church."

"None of us knew about her paintings. The attic where we found them was her private garden." Her grandmother could have never imagined what they would mean to her.

"I'll do all I can to stop this menace, Saul Lance, from destroying Agnes's home and studio. Why, we've never seen anything like this in Worthville before, and as the president of the Worthville Historical Society, we won't have it." Gladiola tapped the purse in her lap for emphasis.

Genny concluded Gladiola might be a force in life as well as in the bowling league. "I was wondering if we could have the depot for a showing this weekend. I know that's short notice, but time is of the essence in this situation."

Gladiola didn't hesitate. "By all means. We have a break between events at the depot, and the town will be ecstatic to see the paintings. I hope we can raise the capital you need."

"I definitely want to give a percentage to the historical society in Grandmother's memory for allowing me to use the facility." Genny thought it the least she could do in exchange for the effort the historical society would be putting forth.

Gladiola nodded. "That's gracious of you. It will be our privilege to be a part of this." She paused a moment, leaned forward, and whispered, "She didn't happen to paint one of Bodine's Bowling Alley, did she?"

"As a matter of fact, she did. From several vantage points."

Gladiola tilted her head back a bit. "Well, then, I know exactly what I'll be buying at the auction."

Genny nodded. "Thank you. I appreciate it so much."

"My pleasure," Gladiola responded and extended her hand. "This is going to be a stellar event."

She shook her hand. "I have every reason to believe it will be. Good-bye, and thanks again." Genny marveled at the contrasts the woman embodied.

Gladiola had another appointment at the depot that afternoon, so she didn't linger and pivioted to exit, which was a blessing since Genny was loaded with patients. Or so she thought.

She checked with Clarice and found two patients had canceled that afternoon. Perfect. That meant she could walk over to David's and tell him the good news about the exhibit. If she was being honest with herself, she knew a phone call would have done the same job. She had to admit she wanted to see David, not just talk to him.

Louvene about hugged the life out of Genny when she went into David's office a couple of hours later. "It's all so wonderful, finding the paintings and saving Agnes's house." Louvene let go, and she could breathe again.

"It is." At last, a way out. Such a relief. She'd been so tense for so long, she was surprised at the way she felt, as if her neck and shoulders wouldn't break anymore when she moved them.

Louvene went on. "I'm going to buy one. When is the exhibit?"

"This weekend at the depot." Gladiola had moved to get the exhibit space fast, making the necessary phone calls just after she left her office. For that, she was grateful.

"I'm spreading the word. There's going to be a mob at the depot this weekend."

If Louvene was going to be her publicity chair, she was even more confident about the outcome of the exhibit. Louvene and her take-charge nature would go a long way in ensuring the success of the showing.

Louvene pushed open David's door and waved for Genny to enter. "Go on in."

Genny entered, but David did not look at her. When he did, he nodded but didn't speak.

Maybe he was having a bad day, but her news was bound to cheer him. She sat down with a flourish. "It's all set for next weekend. I spoke with Gladiola this morning."

"Great," he said, sounding as if he didn't mean it.

She grew concerned. "What is it?"

"I've been thinking."

Oh no. Just like a lawyer. Overanalyzing everything. Why couldn't he put his big brain on hold for a while and enjoy this wonderful turn of events?

"I didn't say anything about this after the fire, because I knew from talking to folks in town that word had gotten out about you giving the money to Al, so if Lance was getting what he wanted, there was no reason to be concerned. But the discovery of the paintings has changed that, and this puts his project in jeopardy. I can't get this off my mind. We're pretty sure Lance burned the shed, but of course, we can't prove it. There's no guessing what else he might be capable of. I want you to be safe."

Genny folded her arms. *What is David saying?*

"You need to understand that not getting this property may bankrupt him. He was counting on this development. If it doesn't go through, he may go under."

Genny tried not to let her suspicious nature take over. Was David taking Lance's side again, or was that just her misjudging him? She fought back the sharp words forming in her mind. Instead, she bit her lip and nodded. "I understand" is all she said.

She stood, managed to say good-bye, and exited, slamming the door a little too hard as she left. A tear of frustration rolled down her cheek. Why couldn't she move past this, once and for all?

After work that evening, she sat at her kitchen table, drinking iced coffee. Through the window, dark clouds formed, threatening rain. The pattern of evening thunderstorms had been disrupted the past few weeks with the dry weather, and they sure needed the rain. But as she sat there, the cloud formation grew more and more ominous.

The stacks of still-packed boxes around her felt a bit ominous too with so much uncertainty hanging in the air. She'd left everything in limbo, not knowing whether she was coming or going.

Literally.

She had every reason to believe the paintings would sell for more than she needed, but she'd called the pod company and asked them not to pick up the pod until the next week in the event something unexpected happened. She put Al and his brothers on standby in case she needed to move out in a hurry. Her thoughts shifted to the situation with David. Was he taking Lance's side again? She took a sip of the coffee, letting the coolness slide down her throat, and found it consoling.

A drop of rain zinged the back window.

Maybe David was truly concerned. Maybe in the end it wasn't David who was at fault here; maybe it was her lack of trust that caused their rifts.

More pellets of rain struck the window. She stood, peering out as the onslaught drenched the thirsty ground. The hydrangea bush just outside was almost visibly revived in the downpour.

The clouds had seemed threatening at first, but she realized it was what was needed to help revive the moisture-deprived earth.

A jagged bolt of light shot to the ground in the distance; then a second or two later came a rumble of thunder.

Though she at times felt threatened by David's comments, maybe she just needed to trust him. Maybe that was the needed component here. But what was holding her back from fully committing?

Another flash of light much closer and almost immediately a crash that shook the house.

She grabbed the counter, her heart rate increasing. That was close.

Once more, she thought about Harriet's words. "She left you a legacy of forgiveness." Perhaps the greatest gift her grandmother had left her was not the paintings but the knowledge that forgiveness is a life-changing, powerful thing. What were those words she underlined?

"Forgiving each other, just as in Christ God forgave you."

CHAPTER THIRTY

G ENNY SURVEYED THE EXHIBIT OF HER grandmother's paintings and thought it a fine tribute to the woman she loved so much.

Gladiola and the Worthville Historical Society took over responsibility for the installation of her grandmother's paintings, which Genny appreciated. With her position at Dr. Fleming's practice, she didn't have time to install a light bulb, much less an art exhibit. When she first discussed the possibility of her leaving with Dr. Fleming, she thought he might cry.

The paintings hung along the walls and on various easels with enough space between them to give the viewer room to consider each one. The historical society placed a number by each painting, and the number corresponded to one on the bid sheets along tables near the entrance. In the silent auction, if you liked a painting, you could add your name to the bid sheet along with the price you wanted to pay. Of course, someone could outbid, which would necessitate monitoring the sheet to see whether the first bidder wanted to raise his or her bid. Each painting also listed a minimum bid the historical society established, which Genny thought to be very generous.

She peered out the depot windows and hoped to see a crowd of folks assembling for the opening, but the street outside was quiet. Too quiet, as if folks were avoiding the area. She checked the flyer hanging on the depot wall to make sure the time and date were right. They were.

David came through the door minutes before the auction began.

It would be best to face what happened between them to avoid awkwardness for the next two hours, but she dreaded it.

She moved toward him, but he spoke first in a quiet voice. "So are we okay?"

She nodded. "I'm sorry I left in such a hurry. It's embarrassing. I really didn't mean to slam the door so hard. Please forgive me."

"Nothing to forgive," he said.

"Yes, there is something to forgive. I... I..."

He put his hand to her lips. "Let's not worry about it right now."

He peered out the window. "I thought we might have a few early shoppers out here."

"I did too. Everyone I spoke with said they were coming."

After a couple of hours standing around in the depot, waiting for customers to come, Gladiola gathered the silent auction sheets and brought them to Genny.

"I'm sorry to say the only bids are mine, Catherine's, and David's."

David looked over Genny's shoulder at the blank auction sheets. "The town must be running scared. I bet Lance put the word out he has more matches. They're afraid Lance will strike out at them if they support you."

Genny's brow furrowed. She couldn't blame them. She saw firsthand what Lance was capable of. "When does the injunction end?"

"Monday."

"I never thought Worthville would be living under such a cloud," Gladiola said with distress in her voice.

Genny sat in a folding chair and put her head in her hands. "I can't sell the paintings by then. It's over." But after a moment, she emerged from self-pity, remembering what she realized in the thunderstorm a few days earlier, gathered herself, stood, and turned to David. "Thanks for everything you did, and I'm sorry for my inappropriate responses. My vision has been clouded."

David hugged her. "I'm sorry things worked out the way they have." David pulled away, defeated. "I guess I'd better go. Are you sure you're all right?"

"I'm fine. Lance won't be coming around. He's gotten what he wants." Genny grabbed her purse and headed out, her grandmother's legacy on her mind.

When she arrived home, she entered and went to the key box. She plucked out the brass key with the red ribbon and held it in her hand. Before she left this house, she needed to tend to some business. Harriet's words again came to mind. "She left you a legacy of forgiveness." She spoke aloud the words her grandmother wrote, the words she'd almost memorized, having read them so many times. "'I'm tired of hating, tired of going over all you took from me. I won't let unforgiveness steal one more second of my life. I'm asking God to help me forgive you once and for all and release this awful bitterness.'"

She was confident her suspicion toward David was connected to the bitterness she felt toward Kurt. While she packed everything else, she didn't want to pack this bitterness once more, as she had when she moved from New York to Worthville. She wanted to let it go. She was sick of it. And like her grandmother, she didn't want to miss the future God planned for her by holding on to her past.

She noted the place where her grandmother's Bible usually lay on the table by the chair. She did something she had done only once in a very long time, when Al asked her to pray for Lori. She dropped her head. "God, please give me the ability to let it all go." When she finished, she grabbed a notepad and pen from a drawer and headed out the back door.

She sat on the steps, put the key beside her, and began writing. "Dear Kurt…"

It took her forty-five minutes to write the letter. She needed to say what he'd done so she could make sure she wasn't still harboring something. "Until recently, I thought your offenses were taking my money, my credit, and breaking my heart. But now, I realize, I also allowed you to take away my ability to trust another man. I allowed you to not only destroy our relationship but any future relationship as well. But that stops today. I will not barricade my heart a moment longer, and I'm asking God to help me take down these walls." Then she wrote the words that up until now had been so impossible to say. "I forgive you." And when she wrote them, she said them out loud. She needed to hear them as well as think them. When she was done, she went outside, gathered a few flowers, and then got in her car and steered it to a long stretch of green grass in town dotted with bouquets and monuments. She left the car and found the marker she was looking for. *Harriet Glaussen*. She knelt and placed a bunch of yellow daisies. "I wanted you to know, Harriet, I did it. I discovered what you meant by a legacy of forgiveness."

And when she stood and moved back to the car, lightness came over her, as if a great weight she'd been carrying lifted at last.

ON MONDAY MORNING GENNY'S phone buzzed as she exited an exam room, and she plucked it from her lab coat. She checked the caller ID before answering. "Hi, David."

"Hi, yourself. Can you come over here during your lunch hour?"

Genny noted the time on her phone—about an hour until she could take off. "What's this about?"

"You'll see," he said.

He sounded mysterious. Her grandmother would have loved it.

She tried to be intentional about not hurrying, but when she finished with her last morning patient, she threw her lab coat across her desk and dashed to David's office. When she entered, Louvene stood smiling in a smug way and waved her toward David's office. He stood behind his desk, also appearing self-satisfied. The clichéd cat that ate the canary came to mind as she studied his demeanor. She shook her head and shrugged. "What's going on?"

David held an eight-by-ten picture of a toothpick on the ground. "You see this?"

Yuck. Why did I walk several blocks to see something this gross? Where is he going with this? "Yes, a disgusting toothpick. It reminds me of someone." She'd never seen Saul Lance when he didn't have a wooden stick hanging from his mouth. And if she never encountered him again with one, it would be fine.

"This is going to be the best moment of your day, maybe of your year—it has been for me."

Genny tried to process what David said. How could a picture of a toothpick do all that? "Enough drama. What are you talking about?"

"Remember the arson investigator? Mr. Lakeland. A while back, I called him and asked if he would take one more look at the case—a lot depended on the outcome. He said he'd be happy to do it, because even though it was for sure arson, he couldn't find any clues leading to who might have done it. When he interviewed Saul Lance, he said those threats he made to you were him blowing off steam. I told him Lance made threats in front of Louvene and me too. So Lakeland kept digging, going over and over the evidence. Then he went out to your place another time. And guess what he found." David wagged the picture of the toothpick in front of Genny. "This toothpick about fifteen feet from the back of your shed."

Genny leaned forward. There'd be no reason for it to be out there. Her grandmother never bought toothpicks. "That's what dental floss is for," she used to say. She was sure neither Al or his dad used them either. At least in public.

David gave her a big grin. "Lakeland thought it odd. The toothpick didn't look old. Ran the DNA." David's chest expanded. "And..." He paused for effect, which was about to drive Genny crazy.

"And?" She was coming out of her skin.

David slapped his knee. "It belongs to Saul Lance. There wouldn't be a reason in this world for Lance to be on your property except he was up to no good."

Genny couldn't believe this.

"But that's not all." David put the toothpick picture on his desk, sat, and put his hands behind his head. "Because his DNA was in the system, it was easy to find Lance is wanted for fraud in Virginia. Had a prior conviction too." David grinned. "We investigated a little and learned Boyle's daughter was the executor of her father's estate, so her signature is on file in the probate court."

David leaned forward as if he was going to pop. "I researched and found the signature does not match the one on the document Lance used to start foreclosure on your house. He forged it." David leaned back again.

"Yes, ma'am, Mr. Lance is in for trouble. The police have a warrant and are at his place right now. Who knows what else they might find?"

"What does all this mean?" There was so much information, Genny was not sure how to tie it all together.

"It means he's not foreclosing on your property, not now, not ever. Judge Stephens dismissed the foreclosure proceeding today."

Genny stood and clapped her hands. "You mean…?"

"I mean you have plenty of time to pay off $20,000. I've already contacted Boyle's daughter, and she's amenable to setting up payments or whatever else you want to do. She was so surprised by the unexpected money, she cried, and she was appalled at Lance's underhanded meanness."

Genny rushed behind the desk and hugged David.

David pointed toward the window, where Genny could see a crowd gathered at the depot. "Louvene put the word out Lance is in jail. I believe you have some patrons who want to see the paintings."

And quite to her surprise, Genny kissed David right there in front of the window for all Worthville to see.

When she pulled away, David's eyes were wide. "Wow, I could get used to that." He grabbed her, pulled her close, and returned the kiss.

Moments later, they strolled across the street to the depot, and as they arrived, Gladiola Spears stepped forward. "Genevieve, I've been appointed to speak for the group." Gladiola looked around at those behind her.

"Everyone wants you to know how sorry they are about the auction. They've brought their checkbooks, and since the paintings are still at the depot, they're ready to buy."

Genny laughed.

Gladiola held a key. "And I have the key to get in." She inserted it into the depot lock, and the crowd piled in behind her.

Al and a little girl in a wheelchair came toward her. Al's eyes conveyed a world of love. "Miss Genny, this here is my granddaughter."

Genny shook Lori's hand. "Pleased to meet you, Lori, and it's good to see you doing so well."

"I'm much better, thank you." She gazed at her grandfather and back to Genny. "I want to see the chicken paintings, Dr. Genny," she said. "But we love the one you gave us of Great-Grandpa mowing the fields. It's beautiful."

Genny pointed in the direction of the door. "You come in. Right this way."

They followed the crowd into the depot, and Genny stood for a moment, relishing all the oohing and ahhing.

Tucker from Tucker's Tomes stood in front of her grandmother's depiction of his place of business. Genny approached and took in how her grandmother painted the store with the illuminated globe in the window. It gave her that feeling of consolation she experienced every time she entered the store. "It's charming, isn't it?"

"Agnes left us all incredible beauty with her amazing talent," Tucker said. Every time he spoke, Genny was transfixed by his voice. She wondered whether he sang opera.

She shook herself. "Yes, yes, she has."

"I plan on outbidding anyone who might make an attempt to buy this painting." He added his substantial bid to the auction sheet with a flourish.

From somewhere in the crowd, "It's my store. It's my store." She followed the cries to where Connie stood ogling a night scene of Connie's Coffee and Cones. The light-up toppings shone in the picture, giving it an almost fairy-tale look. Connie turned to Genny with a tear making a track in her makeup. "When I first started out, I'd saved all the money I could, but I still needed a loan. No banker would give a young single woman with not much credit history money to open a business. But your Agnes believed in me and cosigned the loan. I've worked for years to make the store something this town would be proud of." She looked back at the painting. "I wish she were here so I could thank her one more time."

She spun back around to Genny. "But since she's not, I'm thanking you. You were going through a hard time, but I could never imagine how awful Saul Lance has been to you. Thank God, he's been stopped." Connie took a deep breath. "So here's the deal. From now on, you get half-off coffee and ice cream at Connie's." She put her hand on Genny's arm. "After what you've been through, you could use a little sweetness." Connie penciled a bid in on the painting of her store.

Genny almost fainted at the size of the figure.

Connie winked at her. "Want to make sure no one else outbids me."

CHAPTER THIRTY-ONE

A COUPLE OF WEEKS LATER AT Genny's house, she and David stood by the table, which held the key box. Genny lifted the box. "I've tried to think of the reasons Grandmother kept her painting a secret."

She opened the box. "I wonder if the attic was a special joyous place in the world where she could enjoy the benefits of having forgiven her brother." She pulled out the key with the red ribbon. "Of finding the missing key."

David took the key from her and examined it. "The key that unlocked the studio."

Genny took the key back from him. "And also unlocked her heart and helped her see again." Genny placed the key back in the box. "I want you to know God has helped me forgive Kurt for all he did." She smiled at David.

"And has that unlocked any doors for you, like it did for your grandmother?"

"Well, I haven't felt a sudden urge to pick up a paintbrush, but I am seeing things more clearly." She drew close to David and wrapped her arms around his neck.

David grinned. "I'd love to hear more about your clearer vision. How about let's grab an ice cream cone to discuss it?"

Genny removed her arms from his neck and slipped one through David's arm, and together, they moved to the door as a lawn mower cranked. In a moment, Al whizzed by, grinning from ear to ear perched atop a new riding lawn mower.

David laughed. "I believe Al's enjoying some of the money you received from your grandmother's paintings."

"I didn't use that money for the lawn mower."

"How'd you get it?"

"Traded the car for it." Genny smiled as they got into David's car. As he cranked it to leave, Elizabeth made herself at home on the porch swing. She really needed to get that chicken a henhouse.

That evening when he dropped her off, they lingered on the front porch. The scent of kudzu, hay, and shortleaf pine trees filled the air.

He stroked her hair with his hand. "Remember that day Saul Lance came in?"

"Yes, and you walked out of the office that afternoon, skipping out on an appointment. Louvene was so worried about you, she called me."

He dropped his hand. "Really?"

"Really. So where did you go?"

"I went to the mill. You know, there's a plaque at the Worthville Church dedicating the altar rail to my great-great-grandfather because he was such a man of prayer. That day when I thought you were leaving and everything seemed so dark, I did what I thought Great-Great-Grandfather Worth would have done. I went to the mill and prayed for God to help me either accept the circumstances or change the circumstances. I told Him that what He wanted was more important than what I wanted."

Genny took his hand and squeezed it.

"On the side of that stream, I was able to surrender the tangle of my life in Worthville. I didn't know what the future held, but as the waters moved downstream, I was able to release my concerns with them."

Genny gave him a hug. "And right after that is when everything began falling into place."

"It is, but something is still out of whack for me. There's something I still have to do."

"I understand." Genny could see how the breach with his dad weighed on him.

"I'm going to have to make the first move."

She put her arms around his neck and whispered, "It's going to be okay."

He kissed her cheek and then let go.

"Good night." Genny waved and went inside. She went to the kitchen to get a drink of water, and when she came back, David was still standing on the front porch. He had his cell phone in his hand. She couldn't help but overhear his conversation.

"Dad, if I ever want to have a real life here in

Worthville, I need to make peace with the one I left behind, just like my friend Genny. Who's Genny? Oh, you'd love her. In fact, I think you should meet."

A smile crept across Genny's face as she climbed the stairs for bed.

EPILOGUE

GENNY BUTTONED UP HER COAT. DAVID would be there any minute. She opened the front door, and daffodils opened their happy yellow faces in the front flower bed. Winter was almost over. She'd forgotten how beautiful spring could be in the country. As she was standing there, David pulled into the drive, exited the car, and almost hopped to the front porch. Good mood today. Not that he was often in a bad one. That Saul Lance business last summer had ruffled his feathers a bit, though.

He flashed a smile at her and opened the door. "Ready?"

"I am. Hey, that was some match last night, wasn't it?" They walked to the car, and he held the door open for her.

"Yes, I find it hard to believe you're able to bowl a 192 after only a few months. I'm sure glad I snatched you for our team before the Woodchucks got you. When you slammed the door to my office that day, I thought to myself, *That woman has a powerful arm.* She has to be on my team."

Genny laughed as he closed the door and was glad something good came out of such an awful day. Forgiving Kurt made it the last time her suspicious nature took free rein.

He sat behind the driver's wheel and put the key in the ignition.

"I was a little sad about not playing for the Woodchucks since it was Harriet's team." She grinned at David as she fastened her seat belt. "But I kind of like my teammates on the Wolves." She winked at him. "Where are we going anyway?"

David shook his head. "I'm not telling. You'll have to wait and see."

They left her house, headed toward town, and then, instead of stopping, went to the other side of Worthville and on the outskirts turned north. There was something about this route that was familiar. As Genny and David rolled through the countryside, she spotted a familiar farmhouse, and a man on a mower threw up his straw hat at them. "Wasn't that...?" she started to ask, but David interrupted.

"It was. The man who helped us when we got stuck." He smiled his huge smile. He made a right turn on a road becoming increasing familiar to her.

When they reached what she expected to be a sea of grass, instead she found a well-worn road covered with fresh gravel. David turned the wheel to the right, and as they navigated a curve, Genny's jaw flew open, and she clasped her hands to her mouth.

"You did it! You renovated the mill!"

David smiled again. "I did indeed."

A historically appropriate sign, "Worth's Gristmill," hung on the side of the building. Gone was the knee-high grass, replaced with sod and foundation plantings. Flower boxes adorned the windows. "Everyone in town is going to want to see this.

"If you can believe it, Louvene has known about it all along."

She raised her eyebrows. "Louvene?" Genny found it miraculous the news of the mill renovation hadn't spread like kudzu through Worthville.

"But"—David held up a finger—"I wanted you to be the first to see the finished product." He gave her an adoring look.

Genny put her hand on his shoulder. "Your great-great-grandfather would be so proud of you."

"I hope so," David said.

Genny could hardly wait for the car to come to a rest beside the mill before she flung open the door. She raced to the waterwheel turning freely. She could have stood for hours listening to the water splash over the paddles.

From there, she raced to the mill door. "Let's go in."

"Hold on," David called after her. "You're going to need a key." He reached in front of her and inserted a brass key into the new lock.

When it swung open, Genny almost fainted. The heart-pine floors were brought back to a luster and the milling machinery restored to its former glory. The gears and shafts were clear of cobwebs and dirt.

"Watch this," David said as he turned a lever. The

gears sprang into action. He pointed to the millstone turning.

"Incredible," she said. She moved around the room like a kid at Christmas. "I can't believe you did this without me finding out."

David shook his head. "It wasn't easy. I often stretched the truth to the breaking point." His studied his surroundings. "But it did turn out well, didn't it?"

"It did." An amazing amount of work was accomplished in such a short time. Her grandmother's painting of the old mill hung on the wall. "This is a great before picture, isn't it?"

David nodded. "I'm ever thankful your grandmother didn't forget this place was out here. The contractor I hired was amazed the bones of the structure were in such good condition given the way it was so run-down. He said my ancestor made some excellent choices with the construction." David patted one of the rough-hewn timbers and then pointed to the far wall. "I want to show you this too." He crossed the expansive floor and opened another door.

Genny followed him, and when she stepped outside, she found a simple guesthouse added on the property. She was overcome with the care taken to render it in an architectural style compatible with the mill. "This is beautiful. What a wonderful getaway."

"I thought so." David paused a moment before continuing to fiddle with something in his pocket. "In some of those letters I found in my dad's attic, I read why my great-great-grandfather first came here. He wanted to marry a certain girl but believed he needed to be able to provide for her, so he found a community that needed a gristmill and came here to start one. The girl he had his eye on became my great-great-grandmother."

David dropped to his knee and pulled a ring from his pocket. "You don't need anyone to provide for you, Genny, but I'd like to share all this with you. I love you with all my heart." He looked around him. "We could spend our honeymoon here." He pulled his cell phone from his pocket and held it up to her. "And if it helps, I switched carriers. We have bars now."

Genny laughed. "I love you, too, and I'd marry you with or without bars." She took the ring.

He stood and held her close. They lingered a long time, listening to the water and relishing the legacies that wrapped them both in love.

ABOUT THE AUTHOR

Southern writer, Beverly Varnado is a novelist, screenwriter, and blogger who writes to give readers hope in the redemptive purposes of God.

She has written several novels and a nonfiction memoir, Faith in the Fashion District. One of her screenplays has been a finalist for the prestigious Kairos Prize in Screenwriting and is under option with Elevating Entertainment.

She lives in Georgia with her husband, Jerry, and their chocolate Aussiedor who is outnumbered by several cats. Jerry and Beverly have three children and two grandchildren.

Read her weekly blog One Ringing Bell,
peals of words on faith, living, writing, and art at
oneringingbell.blogspot.com.
Also catch her at www.BeverlyVarnado.com,
on her Facebook author page
https://www.facebook.com/BeverlyVarnadoAuthor
or @VarnadoBeverly

59914126R00155

Made in the USA
Columbia, SC
09 June 2019